"It's not my bride coming here, it's the cleric who'll officiate at the wedding and a representative of her family to witness it."

Revelation was a glare of searing light even as Miranda's vision darkened at the edges. Her breath rattled and she had to drag in more oxygen before attempting to speak.

Zamir beat her to it. Gleaming eyes held hers. He didn't bother concealing his mockery.

"I see you finally understand. How fitting that my bride should be the woman who tried to steal my throne from me and destroy everything our governments have worked for. Who caused this mess in the first place."

He leaned in, invading her personal space so she inhaled that intriguing aroma of cedarwood and virile man.

"*You* will be my bride. We'll marry in an hour."

Growing up near the beach, **Annie West** spent lots of time observing tall, burnished lifeguards—early research! Now she spends her days fantasizing about gorgeous men and their love lives. Annie has been a reader all her life. She also loves travel, long walks, good company and great food. You can contact her at annie@annie-west.com or via PO Box 1041, Warners Bay, NSW 2282, Australia.

Books by Annie West

Harlequin Presents

A Consequence Made in Greece
The Innocent's Protector in Paradise
One Night with Her Forgotten Husband
The Desert King Meets His Match
Reclaiming His Runaway Cinderella
Reunited by the Greek's Baby
The Housekeeper and the Brooding Billionaire
Nine Months to Save Their Marriage

Royal Scandals

Pregnant with His Majesty's Heir
Claiming His Virgin Princess

Visit the Author Profile page
at Harlequin.com for more titles.

Annie West

———

HIS LAST-MINUTE DESERT QUEEN

Recycling programs
for this product may
not exist in your area.

ISBN-13: 978-1-335-59322-1

His Last-Minute Desert Queen

Copyright © 2024 by Annie West

For questions and comments about the quality of this book,
please contact us at CustomerService@Harlequin.com.

Harlequin Enterprises ULC
22 Adelaide St. West, 41st Floor
Toronto, Ontario M5H 4E3, Canada
www.Harlequin.com

Printed in U.S.A.

HIS LAST-MINUTE DESERT QUEEN

To those readers who adore a desert romance and asked me for more.

There are too many of you to mention individually but I want to thank you so much for your enthusiasm!

Zamir and Miranda's story is for you.

CHAPTER ONE

ZAMIR PINCHED THE bridge of his nose as he stepped from the air-conditioned luxury of the hotel foyer into searing sunlight that heightened his hammering headache. Only then did he realise he'd forgotten his sunglasses.

The last few days hadn't been long enough to fit in all he needed to do. But—the thought shimmered like the promise of life-giving water in the desert—by the end of today it would all fall into place.

He breathed a sigh of exhausted satisfaction. The last weeks had been hell but he hadn't allowed himself time to mourn. He'd had to be strong for his family and his country. Now he was on the cusp of achieving everything he'd promised his dying uncle.

Securing the crown and therefore the stability of his homeland, Qu'sil.

And paving the way to reunify Qu'sil and neighbouring Aboussir into one nation.

There'd be celebrations across both countries when it was done. Even the most diehard nationalists in both places had agreed this was the way forward. But negotiating a balance that gave equal weight to both sides had been time-consuming and tough.

Now there was just one last item to tick off and everything could proceed.

The most crucial item of all.

Without breaking stride, holding his phone to his ear as his finance minister detailed an unforeseen budget problem, Zamir strode to the waiting limo.

The car door was open, held by a chauffeur standing to attention. Zamir's brow twitched as he wondered why his hosts should insist the driver wear gloves, unnecessary in this heat, without ensuring his uniform fitted. Even his hat seemed too big, shadowing his face.

But Zamir had other things on his mind. With murmured thanks to the driver, he got in and focused on his minister, stretching out his legs and reaching for sparkling water.

A few minutes later he ended the call and took one from his head of royal security. Hassan hadn't liked him travelling without his usual escort in a foreign country, even on this short trip from the hotel. But that was the point. For Zamir to show complete trust in his hosts and the people of Aboussir who would, once the legalities were completed, be his subjects.

'Relax, Hassan. I'm on my way. I'll see you soon.' He looked out at the crowded, narrow streets of the old city, where traffic moved at a snail's pace. 'Don't worry if I'm a little late. The roads here aren't as streamlined as at home.' A small laugh escaped. 'At least they won't start the ceremony without me.'

Ending the call, he frowned at his phone then pressed the button to lower the privacy screen between himself and the driver.

Despite the tinted windows, the sunlight made him squint. The medication he'd taken for his headache hadn't yet kicked in. He took another long swig of water. He should have taken time for a proper breakfast but despite all the preparations, his uncle's death had meant a flurry of work.

But soon… After today, Zamir could at least take the night off.

'My phone battery is low,' he said to the driver. 'I need to charge it.' Something he usually did before sleeping but there'd been no sleep last night.

'Of course, sire.'

Sire? Such an old-fashioned word but then Aboussir was more traditional than his country. There most addressed him as sir. Soon, after being formally acclaimed Sheikh and Head of State, it would be Majesty.

Zamir's mouth tugged down. He'd known that day was coming, that his uncle couldn't last for ever, yet he missed the old man.

'If you pass me the phone, sire, I'll see to it.'

The man's voice was light, very young by the sound of it.

As long as he knew the way, that was all that mattered. But he manoeuvred his way deftly between vehicles, livestock and pedestrians.

'Thank you.' Zamir passed the phone over and sat back, closing his eyes against a sudden swimming sensation. He really should have snatched some rest. 'How long till we get there? Fifteen minutes?'

'Longer, I'm sorry. There's been a major accident. We'll have to detour off the main road. But I'll get you where you need to be.'

Zamir nodded but didn't open his eyes. This appointment was vital. He'd power nap now, ready to be at his best.

* * *

Even as she drove the air-conditioned vehicle, Miranda's skin was clammy, not from the temperature but nerves.

Nerves? More like outright terror!

Even for her, the one labelled so often by her family as volatile and irresponsible, today's actions were beyond the pale.

How had she ever thought she'd succeed? It had been an act born of desperation. Not her desperation but her cousin's. Miranda couldn't turn her back on Sadia in her distress.

When she'd come up with the plan she'd been more than half joking but Sadia had jumped at the idea. For once her timid cousin wasn't concerned with propriety or repercussions.

Why would she worry when you're taking all the risks?

That was unfair. Sadia couldn't do this. She'd have been missed if she'd sneaked out this morning. Anyway, if this came undone they'd both pay.

Correction, they'd both pay anyway, whether Miranda succeeded or not. There'd be no hiding what they'd done.

Her breath caught, her brain atrophying at the thought of what would happen if they succeeded. Even her fertile imagination couldn't picture it.

But if they succeeded it would be worth whatever repercussions were meted out. To sit idle and let Sadia down was impossible. They'd been friends all their lives, even through the years of Miranda's absence from Aboussir.

Swinging the big car through an archway into the new part of the city, she glanced in the rear-view mirror.

He looked asleep, shoulders resting against the cushioned backrest, long limbs sprawled and head to one side.

He was the most imposing man she'd ever seen. The photos didn't do him justice, even though they showed a broodingly handsome man. There was something about him in the flesh, a confidence, an aura of—elemental masculinity were the only words to describe it—that turned the air around him electric and made her janglingly aware of her own sex.

Given that she'd spent so much time around men, often good-looking men with never a qualm, that awareness shocked her.

A shiver scuttled down her backbone. It was one thing to hatch this outrageous plan, huddled in Sadia's room at midnight. It was another to carry it out.

Her courage had taken a battering when she'd read about Sheikh Zamir's sharp intellect and his prowess both in government and in any athletic endeavour. The press painted him as someone who could look after his country and himself, no matter what the circumstances. It wouldn't be easy to best such a man.

Her cursory research last night had left her worried, wishing she could pull out of this hare-brained scheme. But Sadia was desperate.

Miranda felt guilty, wishing Sadia hadn't left it until the last minute to seek help, knowing she'd be almost thankful if the plan failed. But it hadn't and she'd found herself frozen with a dreadful mix of fear and excitement as Sheikh Zamir strode out to the car.

Her heart had risen to her throat as she took in the big man's lazy yet purposeful gait. The breadth of his shoulders beneath his traditional robe. His well-shaped, powerful hands. And the glitter of ebony eyes in a hard, handsome face that made her insides squirm.

Miranda's stepfather was handsome, like many of his polo-playing friends. She was used to good-looking sportsmen who moved as if they owned the world.

But Sheikh Zamir was in a class of his own.

Ignoring the heat coursing through her at the thought, she turned onto the main road out of the city, casting a quick look in the rear-vision mirror, but he hadn't moved. Her heartbeat quickened as she accelerated, waiting for that deep voice to ask why they were heading away from their destination.

No protest came. Maybe he really was asleep.

Yet she felt nauseous with worry.

They left the built-up area. Another look in the mirror and this time she caught him moving, not sitting up to demand where they were going but snuggling deeper into the leather seat. The contrast between his severe, ultra-masculine features and that tiny movement, as if seeking comfort, sent a spiral of something unfamiliar through her middle.

Her breath escaped in a gusty sigh of relief.

She checked the time. It felt as if she'd been driving for hours but if she turned the car around now they'd hardly even be late.

Setting her jaw, Miranda focused on the road and all the reasons she was doing this.

Because she hated bullies. Because Sadia was too precious to be treated this way. Because, come what may, disgrace, international incident, maybe even imprisonment, what this man planned was wrong. It might be Sadia's father actually forcing her to comply, but it was at the behest of *this* man. If no one else had the courage to stand up to him, Miranda had to.

The car approached an intersection of three highways. Miranda darted a look towards the back seat then opened her window a sliver. In one quick move she grabbed his phone and dropped it out.

There. If someone tried to locate him using his phone, they'd have no chance.

If only she'd thought to do it while they were in the city. Then anyone pursuing them wouldn't know if they were still in the metropolis.

Miranda smiled shakily. She'd make a mental note.

In case she ever kidnapped a royal sheikh again.

CHAPTER TWO

ZAMIR'S MIND FELT dull and there was a bad taste in his mouth. That medication! He'd used it only once before, years ago, and had forgotten how lethargic it left him.

At least his head wasn't pounding any more. He'd take that as a win.

Then he realised the car had stopped. He snapped his eyes open, disliking the idea of being found dozing instead of alert, ready for this important occasion.

It took long moments to digest what he saw.

There was no chauffeur, no welcoming host, no familiar faces from his entourage. Instead of the entrance to a palace and eager faces, he looked onto stony ground that dropped down to a plain. There were no buildings and the only road a gravel track that disappeared around a hillock.

His nape pinched tight and he tensed. Clearly they'd left the city but where he was, he had no idea.

He strained to hear any telltale sound. A voice, a footfall. A gun being cocked.

The height of the sun told him hours had elapsed since he left his hotel. Whatever had happened, the driver had been part of it. At least the man had left the car open and the windows down, in the growing heat.

He swung his head around and realised the vehicle was parked in the shade. Behind rose a tall stone wall with high, shuttered windows.

Zamir's heart thudded. Where was he?

Uncoiling from the car, he rose, balanced on the balls of his feet, only a little unsteady, ready to face an attack.

None came. He stood listening, but there was nothing except the sigh of an afternoon breeze rounding the massive wall. What was this place?

More to the point, why was he here?

He allowed himself a single flicked glance at his watch, confirming what he knew. He was hours late for his appointment.

Hassan would be frantic. Not just Hassan. The whole machinery of the royal court would swing into emergency mode when he didn't arrive.

Bending to the front window, he confirmed what he'd feared. His phone had disappeared. Nevertheless he searched thoroughly. Nothing.

Zamir's jaw set and his gut curdled as he considered the consequences of missing today's appointment. It was catastrophic.

What enemy of the state had planned this?

Why leave him, alone and unharmed? This bizarre situation turned stranger by the moment.

Swiftly, keeping in the shadow of the building, he ran silently down the length of the wall, pausing at the corner. Still he saw no one but on this side was an entrance. A huge arched entrance with stout wooden doors, studded with iron and ornate, antique hinges. The sort of doors designed to keep marauders out. His own palace had something similar, though grander and in better repair.

The notable thing here was that one of them stood open. In invitation or oversight?

Scooping up a fist-sized rock from the barren ground, Zamir moved forward.

Miranda's hands shook so badly even now that she had to pause and take deep breaths.

He'd be okay. He was just asleep. Yet when she'd tried to wake him he hadn't moved.

Because you barely dared touch him.

Because, once he wakes, you'll have to face the consequences of what you've done.

It worried her that she'd had to leave him outside in the afternoon heat, because her genius plan hadn't factored in his sheer size. Well over six feet and strongly muscled, he was too big for her to move.

She gripped the bench and told herself he'd be fine. It wasn't midsummer, when the temperatures rose lethally in the desert. There was a breeze passing through the car and she'd take water and a wet cloth to cool him.

As soon as her fumbling fingers managed the stiff catch on the bathroom cupboard.

She'd never expected he'd sleep so long. With every kilometre out of the city she'd expected him to wake and demand she turn around. She'd never believed the plan would work.

At least Sadia was safe. Miranda tried to convince herself that was all that mattered.

She swiped damp hands down the bulky uniform jacket and reached again for the cupboard. Finally she managed to open it and reached in, when the flesh between her shoulder blades tingled and her breath stopped.

She wasn't alone.

There'd been no sound but she *felt* the difference.

'Withdraw your hand slowly and turn around.'

Fear rose to a point just this side of panic at the harsh authority in that rough voice.

Heart hammering, Miranda turned her head.

It was the Sheikh, very much alive. He bristled with energy, narrowed eyes glittering in a way that made her breath stop then start again, painfully as if her lungs forgot how to work.

His obsidian-black gaze raked her, her flesh stinging as if he'd grazed it. Didn't they make razor-sharp knives from volcanic obsidian?

She swallowed convulsively, the movement painful as she felt that sharpness in her throat.

His handsome, brooding features were set like a granite thundercloud. His eyes were narrowed, his mouth grim and nostrils flared disdainfully.

His shoulders filled the doorway and even from a couple of metres away he mastered the space, sucking the oxygen out.

Every protective instinct urged Miranda to run or hide. Except there was nowhere to hide and he blocked the only door.

She drew a shuddering breath.

Time to face the music.

He ruled a kingdom, would soon rule two, and no doubt was used to having his every wish obeyed. He was powerful and incensed. She could hardly blame him, after what she'd done.

'I—'

'Let me see what you've got in your hand. Slowly.'

Miranda nodded, the too-large cap slipping further down her forehead as she pulled her arm from the cupboard. But the braid at the wrist snagged on that troublesome catch, stopping her. She lifted her other hand to free the fabric.

She was still struggling with it when something collided with her, pivoting her back against the wall.

Stunned, she felt the world dim, blocked out by the tall body pinioning her. She dragged in a desperate breath, discovering it scented with cedarwood and warm spice.

Then she heard that same deep voice, muttering something she couldn't catch.

There was movement, the weight against her eased a fraction, resolving itself into the solid torso of Sheikh Zamir of Qu'sil as he pulled back just enough to survey her.

Miranda sucked in another lungful of desperate air. She'd thought him imposing and haughty. This close she discovered something else in that austere face that made her, for one confusing moment, forget they were enemies.

'A woman?'

There was no need to answer. He knew the shape of her breasts and hips now just as she knew the breadth of his chest, the jut of his narrow hip bones and the power in those long, encompassing legs. The ferocious heat of him seared into her.

Miranda blinked up at a jaw so sharply squared she was mesmerised. Or maybe that was shock. She'd imagined the Sheikh as a distant figure, a problem to be overcome. Not a man, potently alive, whose body against hers evoked unaccustomed responses.

'I was kidnapped by a woman?'

He plucked off her cap. For a pulse beat, and another and yet another, he stared at her cropped curls.

His narrowed eyes flared.

Slowly he loosened his grip on her wrist. Pins and needles prickled, making her gasp and flex stiff fingers.

'You were going to attack me with a *towel*?'

He unwrapped the towel she'd been holding when her arm got snagged and she used his distraction to try wriggling free. But he was having none of that, holding her where she was with disturbing ease.

Miranda gulped. There was nothing sexual about what he did. Yet a single spark of heat swirled through her pelvis and remained there, warm against the chill enveloping her.

She cleared her throat. 'Of course I wasn't going to attack you. I was getting a towel.'

'There's no of course about it.'

His eyes met hers and her breath went AWOL again. Fear could do that. It had nothing to do with the strange *awareness* she felt.

Of them not as kidnapped and kidnapper, but as male and female.

Her breathing quickened and he eased back a little more.

'Where are your accomplices?'

'I don't have any.'

It wasn't a lie. Sadia knew the plan, had helped devise it, but it was Miranda alone who'd carried it out. Even now she could barely believe she'd got away with it for so long.

Maybe she hadn't. Maybe this was a crazy dream and she'd wake soon.

Except this man was too real. Even her fertile imagination couldn't have conjured up someone like him.

'What are you smiling at?'

'I'm not smiling. I'm dazed.'

His forbidding expression didn't ease. 'That's my line. I'm the one you kidnapped. What were you doing here?'

Miranda chewed the corner of her mouth. 'I worried when you didn't wake. I was getting water for you and a towel to wet.'

'Tending to my needs? You're a regular Florence Nightingale, aren't you?'

Miranda held his fulminating stare. 'I was worried you might be unwell.' She swallowed hard. 'But I'm not sorry I kidnapped you.'

Zamir watched her chin lift in an attitude of defiance that should have been laughable.

It wasn't. Instead it intrigued.

He might even have labelled her absurd attitude engaging if it weren't for the catastrophe she'd caused.

He felt her runaway pulse yet she kept her cool. She was brave, he'd give her that.

But how dangerous was she? And who else did he have to contend with?

'If you wouldn't mind, I'd like to stand alone now.'

There it was again, that courageous insouciance as if she weren't bothered by the fact that she was now at *his* mercy.

He scrutinised her, from the gaping collar of her obviously borrowed or stolen uniform to the nimbus of mahogany hair like a sexy, dark halo. Her skin was fine-grained, a pale olive-gold that contrasted bewitch-ingly with eyes of light grey-blue.

Bewitchingly? That medication must be impairing his thoughts.

Her features were unremarkable yet pleasing. Or they would be if she hadn't single-handedly destroyed every-thing he and so many others had worked for.

On a surge of furious energy Zamir stepped back, watching as she straightened her jacket and moved away from the wall. He could have frisked her to be com-pletely sure she had no concealed weapons, but he'd touched enough of her to believe she was no immedi-ate threat.

Nevertheless, he positioned himself beside the open doorway where he could see anyone approach. 'Why are we here? Who are we meeting?'

'We're not meeting anyone.'

She arched her back, one hand to her shoulder blade. The movement thrust her breasts against the jacket, re-minding him, as if he weren't already fully aware, that she was a young, attractive woman.

Assassins and fanatics came in all shapes and sizes, he reminded himself. He was attuned not only to her movements but to the silence beyond this room, antici-pating the arrival of her partners in crime.

'Then why are we here?'

'I needed somewhere to take you that's off the grid so you can't get back quickly to the city.' She stood tall. 'There's no phone. I know you won't believe me, but it's true. I threw yours away.'

Zamir would indeed check for himself. 'And now you have me here? Who's making the ransom demand?'

Dark eyebrows pinched above those bright eyes.

'There is no ransom demand. I've done what I set out to do.' She looked at the man's watch on her slender wrist. 'You've missed the ceremony and it's too late to return, that's all that matters.'

She was right. That was all that mattered.

Even now Zamir couldn't believe how such a promising day had ended in disaster. The headache that had plagued him this morning began pounding anew. If he had time to waste he'd berate her over the unthinkable damage she'd done.

But she knew what she'd done. It was there in those wary, pewter-bright eyes.

'Who are you working for?'

His country didn't have enemies as such but some were jealous of its phenomenal financial successes. Perhaps too, some envied its stability and social harmony and the way it was held up as an example to others. That success would increase when Qu'sil and Aboussir rejoined.

Except that reunion might no longer be possible. Time was running out. Thanks to this woman. He gritted his teeth.

'I told you. No one.'

His pulse drummed painfully in his temple as he clung to a veneer of patience. Exhaling slowly, he held out his hand. 'I'll have the car keys now.'

She swallowed and moistened her bottom lip.

He'd swear it was an instinctive gesture, and it made him revise his assessment that her face was unremarkable but for those eyes. Now her cupid's bow mouth and especially her fuller, sensual bottom lip held his gaze. His body temperature hiked up a couple of degrees.

'You can't. The first thing I did was throw the keys

down the well in the courtyard. I can't afford for you to get back to the capital today.'

She didn't sound defiant now. Was she belatedly realising how vulnerable her position?

Yet she must have some protection apart from sheer bravado. She clearly expected his wrath after what she'd done.

The ruler of Qu'sil outwitted and abducted by a woman in her early twenties!

It was laughable. Preposterous.

Cataclysmic.

Because it wasn't simply his pride on the line. It was his nation's future.

Zamir stepped forward and she shuffled back, bringing him up short.

Not so brazen now. Uncertain, but trying not to look it with her chin still angled high.

'How far to the nearest habitation?'

'Too far to walk. It would be dark before you got there and you'd probably lose the track and get lost. I doubt there are any torches here. Not that you'll believe me.'

He nodded. He didn't believe her.

But the view through the window behind her seemed to confirm what she said. Nevertheless he'd have to try. After he'd checked for a hidden phone. He couldn't imagine she'd come here without some form of communication.

Zamir folded his arms. This *was* an ideal place to hide a captive. He suspected they were in the remote area near the border of their two countries. But instinct told him there had to be another reason she'd brought him here.

'What is this place? *Whose* is it?'

'It's mine. But I haven't been here in years.'

In a day of surprises she still managed to confound him.

'Yours?'

The size of the place and the faded grandeur he'd seen so far pointed to it being an old fortress palace, albeit neglected.

She nodded, seeming to find his collar inordinately fascinating. Because she was, finally, realising she no longer had the upper hand? But then, as if she were reading his thoughts, her head snapped up, those startling, misty eyes meeting his.

He dismissed the zap of energy he felt as their gazes locked.

'I inherited it from my father but no one has lived here for a while.'

Zamir rocked back on his heels then forward. 'How convenient to have somewhere isolated enough to hold a kidnap hostage.'

She scowled. 'You're not a hostage. And I didn't *know* I was going to kidnap you. It was only last night—'

She stopped and bit her lip.

'It was a last-minute plan?' His eyes narrowed. Could it be true? Had he been outwitted by a woman who'd acted on the spur of the moment? He refused to believe it. 'Ms…?'

'Fadel. Miranda Fadel.'

Zamir stiffened, his scant amusement at her lies fading. He knew that name, knew it very well. If she were indeed from that family…

'You're related to Sadia Fadel?'

She nodded, her features taut. Her expression persuaded him this at least was no lie. 'She's my cousin. We grew up together.'

She licked her lip again as if her mouth were dry. Once more Zamir felt an echo of heat low in his body but was too shocked to focus on it.

'You're also related to the Sheikh of Aboussir?'

It was the Sheikh, with Zamir's uncle, then Sheikh of Qu'sil, who had proposed today's ceremony. If he'd changed his mind he would have told Zamir, not concocted this outrageous kidnap.

'Distantly. The Sheikh's cousin had two sons. Sadia's father is the elder and my father was the younger.'

Zamir nodded. He knew the family tree. The fact that the Sheikh of Aboussir had no children made his cousin's children his closest relatives. That had been one of the reasons he'd felt free to support an amalgamation of their countries. Sadia's father, the Sheikh's distant, surviving male relative, wasn't considered suitable to rule. The two royal Sheikhs and their governments had agreed that Zamir would rule both nations, once his position was confirmed with his marriage.

The marriage that had been due to take place today.

Because the laws of his own nation decreed that the royal Sheikh, if not already married, should wed within three weeks of his predecessor's death or be passed over in favour of a married man.

An arranged marriage between himself as heir to one throne and Sadia Fadel from the royal family of Aboussir had been devised. Both royal families would combine to create a new dynasty to rule over the new nation.

The original plan had been for the wedding to take place in several months' time with the blessing of both ruling Sheikhs. Except Zamir's beloved uncle, ill for so long, had suddenly taken a turn for the worse, dying mere weeks ago.

The last thing Zamir wanted now was to consider marrying. His grief and his nation's were enough to cope with. Except it *had* to be done, quickly, and the wedding had been brought forward to today.

'Why?' He glared. 'Why wreck what we've all worked towards?'

'All? Don't you mean you and Sadia's father, my uncle? *He's* the one who wanted this wedding. He wants his daughter married to a powerful sheikh. He can't rule so he wants to be close to the man who does. All this is just about personal power and influence.'

The repugnance in her tone matched the curl of her lip and Zamir was torn between disbelief and fascination. His character, hard work and dedication were known to all. He was a man of principle who'd devoted his life to his country, not for personal gain but because it was his duty.

'What can I possibly have done to warrant that sneer?'

He should be pressing for more details of the plot, yet he was distracted by her dismissal. The insult to his integrity was like a sneaking stab to the gut.

What did she think gave *her* the right to judge *him*?

'You really don't know?' She shook her head. 'You try to force a woman into marriage and think it's all right? Because you're greedy enough to want to rule two nations instead of one.'

'Force?' Zamir strode closer, compelled into movement by her outrageous suggestion. 'I've used no force!

You'll have to produce a better lie than that. What's your real motive? Who do you work for?'

Instead of being cowed as he towered over her, the woman had the nerve to stare right back, jaw set and eyes flashing. Only the quick rise and fall of her breasts beneath the drab uniform betrayed her disquiet.

'Of course it was to be a forced marriage.' She paused. 'Your bride told me.'

CHAPTER THREE

MIRANDA SLUMPED BACK against the wall, knees drawn up to her chest and mind racing.

She didn't wear a watch so couldn't be sure of the time, but it seemed hours since they'd heard a vehicle approaching. That had galvanised Sheikh Zamir into action. He'd hurried her through the building until he found a bare storeroom with a solid lock.

At one point she'd heard voices, deep male voices, but then they moved away and there was only silence.

What was he doing? Why had he left her here so long? And who had arrived? No one knew where they were.

Miranda recalled the Sheikh's expression when she'd called him out for forcing Sadia into marriage. Indignation and fury, and something else that had looked almost like surprise.

She'd put that down to the fact no one had ever had the temerity to confront him about his methods. Yet when he'd questioned her again and she'd confirmed Sadia herself had told her she was being forced into the marriage, that she was petrified at the prospect of marrying a stranger and becoming a queen, he'd looked astounded.

Again and again she circled back to that moment, unable to shake the conviction that something was wrong.

Apart from the fact that you kidnapped a head of state and now have to face the consequences?

Her mouth turned down as her blood iced. She could barely imagine her uncle's ire.

But it wasn't her uncle she needed to worry about, not yet. In her hasty planning, she'd had no time to think about what came next. She'd been so focused on achieving the impossible, delaying the Sheikh long enough to prevent the wedding, that she'd been hazy on the aftermath.

She'd assumed that once they arrived here she'd hide the car keys and, when enough time had passed, she'd drive them back to the city. That was before she saw Sheikh Zamir in the flesh and realised only the most drastic action would keep him from his appointment.

His boldness, his air of determination and unmistakable power had made her rethink.

Miranda had realised she could take no chances. She'd ditched the car keys where he couldn't retrieve them, just as she'd had to dispose of his phone.

Which meant she was trapped here as he was.

Her thoughts snagged on the memory of his hard frame pressing her against the wall.

Never in her twenty-three years had she been so close to a man, so *aware* of him. It had been the strangest sensation, anxiety mixing with something that even now made her blood pulse quicker.

Pinpricks had peppered her body and she'd assumed it was reaction to his anger. But she'd faced anger before. Her uncle had never approved of her and had found fault with her since childhood. Yet Miranda had never experienced anything like today's phenomenon.

Her thoughts began another, useless cycle of regret, fear and determination, when she heard the key grate in the lock. By the time the door swung open she was standing on wide-braced feet, her back to the wall.

A strongly built man in a dark, tailored suit surveyed her, his expression blank.

'His Highness will see you now.'

His Highness. Whoever this man was, he was an ally of Sheikh Zamir. So much for her fragile hope that the new arrival was someone who might help her.

She had no allies. No powerful ones anyway, though she had a few friends back in the city. Her parents were dead and though she'd spent most of her early life in Aboussir it had been years since she'd lived here.

Miranda swallowed, her mouth dry and throat scratchy, and felt the wall press against her shoulder blades. Then she gathered her tattered courage and stepped forward. He waited until the last moment to allow her to exit.

He shadowed her every step, a forbidding gaoler.

It was almost reassuring to enter one of the sitting rooms and see the familiar figure of Sheikh Zamir standing with his back to her, looking out the window.

The fluttery sensation of relief was surely misplaced. He was her enemy.

He turned swiftly, robe flaring wide, frowning eyes homing in on hers. She was reminded of a hawk, its wings outspread, piercing gaze already locked on its hapless prey.

For long seconds he pinioned her with that fierce stare, making her wonder how far this man would go for revenge. One thing was for sure, he wasn't used to being crossed. He was used to ordering and being obeyed.

He'd ordered a suitable bride and expected her meek compliance.

The thought of Sadia settled her churning stomach a little. Miranda knew he'd make her suffer for what she'd done but it was worth it if Sadia remained free.

'You can leave us, Hassan. You have things to organise and Ms Fadel and I have matters to discuss.'

The other man turned away, his footsteps silent.

That was a feat Sheikh Zamir had managed too. She tried to ease her tension by telling herself it was something they must teach in Qu'sil. Yet her heart beat too fast and she felt the panicked urge to run from his gimlet stare.

When her nerves had finally reached screaming point he spoke.

'Sit.'

He gestured to a low divan while he sank onto its mate near the window.

Miranda was tempted to say she preferred to stand but her wobbly knees might give way. She refused to let him see how stressed she was.

For a second she considered making a run for it. But where would she go? Besides, for all his air of stately command, she'd come in close contact with his fit, powerful body. He'd reach her before she escaped the room. Plus there was his hulky bodyguard. She'd never evade them both.

On stiff legs she crossed to the divan and sank creakily, every joint stiff. She hadn't slept last night, had spent the previous day travelling back to Aboussir, and stress had finally hit her like a sledgehammer.

Stress and fear. She was about to face the consequences of her actions.

She recalled, almost with fondness, the way her uncle used to rant at her reckless actions as a kid. He'd bluster and lock her in her room and take away privileges. But this was different. She was no longer a confused kid and, apart from his disapproval, this man was nothing like her uncle. He didn't rant, just surveyed her with a hooded, intense gaze that made her wonder exactly what the legal penalty was for kidnapping a sheikh.

Miranda tried to divert her morbid thoughts. 'He works for you, I take it?' Her voice was unsteady. 'How did he find you?'

For a second she thought he wouldn't answer, then his mouth flicked up at one corner in cool amusement.

'What you didn't realise when you tossed my phone was that the car was one supplied by His Majesty the Sheikh of Aboussir for today's ceremony. All royal vehicles are fitted with GPS trackers, though it took some hours before Hassan learned that and was able to follow.'

A while. How long?

She looked at the patch of sky beyond his broad shoulder. It was almost dark. Surely there was no time to return to the city and force Sadia into marriage.

'You claim you acted alone. You also claim your sole purpose was to prevent your cousin being forced into marriage.' He grimaced on the word *forced*. 'What about the other consequences of your actions?'

'Other consequences?'

Wasn't it enough that she'd stopped the wedding?

She *hoped* she'd stopped the wedding. When the Sheikh didn't arrive there'd be uproar and in the aftermath Sadia would hopefully persuade her parents it would be better if she left until the scandal blew over.

The Sheikh leaned back against a row of silk cushions and it struck Miranda as ominous that he didn't seem in a rush to leave.

Given the luxurious setting and his semi-reclining pose, he should have looked like a louche sybarite. But those hawkish, handsome features were too intent, too focused.

He'd always attract women. No doubt he had them queuing for his attention, not simply because of his wealth and power but because of his undeniable charisma. It horrified her that she noticed. More than noticed. She felt an undercurrent of sexual awareness tug her lower body.

Miranda froze, pulse skittering at her body's betrayal. It was so wrong. The man was her enemy.

'The crown of Qu'sil.'

She shook her head, trying to focus on his words. 'Sorry? What about the crown of Qu'sil?'

One hand lazily stroked a crimson silk cushion but there was no softening of his expression. 'The fact that I need to marry in order to become Sheikh.'

Miranda started. 'I don't understand.'

Silence reigned. A silence in which those black eyes bored into hers as if reading every weakness, every doubt.

'Who persuaded you to kidnap me? It must be someone with political ambitions to control my country.'

'Not that again. I told you I acted alone.'

'You'd have me believe it's sheer bad luck that, because of you, I'll be unable to become Sheikh of Qu'sil, the position I've trained for since the age of ten?'

She scowled. 'But you *are* the Sheikh.'

Slowly he shook his head. 'I'm acting in the role, have been since my uncle's illness took a turn for the worse. But I'm not officially Sheikh yet. Nor will I be unless I marry.'

'Oh.' She sat back, her mind spinning. 'So today's wedding wasn't just about taking over Aboussir too.'

It was amazing how eyes so dark could glitter so brightly. Yet despite his banked fury, his voice was cool. 'You make me sound like a power-hungry desperado, instead of the man chosen by both nations to be leader.'

That was news, but then Miranda had been living overseas, not following politics here. All she knew was what Sadia had told her. Which, she began to realise, wasn't much.

'So, you need a bride to become Sheikh.'

It seemed implausible but he clearly wasn't joking. Hauteur turned his features grim. Grim, coldly angry and still undeniably sexy.

Miranda shivered and told herself she was imagining things. Maybe she was sickening with something. A fever might explain the heat coursing through her body, the trembling, the fact that even now, about to face whatever punishment he meted out, she couldn't keep her tongue between her teeth. If she could pretend to be meek and biddable, or at least apologetic, things might go more easily.

Who was she trying to kid? Easy wasn't in this man's lexicon. And to be duped by a lone woman, that must be a blow to his precious pride. She wasn't naïve enough to expect mercy.

A taut smile curled his mouth. He spread his arms wide, resting them on the back of the cushions, the image of ease. Except for those burning eyes.

'Fortunately I have a back-up plan, since time is of the essence.'

'It is?'

Why was he sitting, telling her this when he could be driving back to the capital? The more she pondered, the less she liked this situation. Her nape drew tight, prickling with foreboding.

But how could this situation get worse? She'd already been caught red-handed.

'Yes, a new Sheikh of Qu'sil must be married or, if not, must wed within three weeks of their predecessor's death or abdication.' His smile deepened yet Miranda discerned no amusement in it. 'To secure the succession, you understand.'

Mutely she stared back. She wished he'd just tell her what her punishment was and get it over.

'Today is my deadline.'

His words fractured her thoughts. She blinked, turning them over, trying to read another meaning into them. 'You mean,' she said slowly, understanding dawning, 'you have to marry *today*? Or you can't be Sheikh?'

He inclined his head, his mouth flat.

Miranda's eyes locked on the sky through the window, now turning indigo.

What had she done?

It was one thing to save her cousin. She couldn't regret that. But had she changed the course of politics? Could she have denied this man the chance to rule his country?

Last night she'd tried to discover what he was like as a person. She'd got the impression he'd played a key part in his country's recent successes and modernisation. He was supposed to be capable and powerful. He didn't suffer fools and he had a reputation for aloofness but also competence.

She waited for him to say she misunderstood.

He didn't. He sat there, still and dour and judgemental, and her heart sank.

'You're serious.' She swiped her tongue around dry lips and swallowed. 'I had no idea. I'm sorry. I—'

'It doesn't matter whether you're sorry.' He didn't raise his voice. He spoke softly and low yet the sound chilled her to the marrow. 'What matters is fixing this before it's too late.'

'You're serious? You really do have a back-up plan?' She frowned. 'Why are you here talking to me? Why aren't you heading back to do whatever needs to be done?'

'There's no need.' She heard a thread of satisfaction in that deep voice. 'The final scene in this catastrophe will play out right here.'

'Your man, Hassan. He's organising it?' Whatever it was.

'Very astute of you, Ms Fadel. He is indeed. In another hour it should all be done.'

She racked her brains. 'You're marrying here?' She looked around the room that hadn't been redecorated in decades. Once luxurious, it was faded and dusty.

'It's appropriate given the connection with my bride's family.'

Miranda shot to her feet, wobbling on unsteady legs. 'You're going to force Sadia, even after all this? Even knowing she doesn't want to marry you?'

No mistaking the flash of distaste on his aristocratic features.

That was why he'd taken the time to explain it to her.

He wanted her to understand what was happening and know she'd failed.

He got to his feet in a single, graceful movement that brought him too close for comfort, yet she refused to step back.

'It was agreed I'd marry into the royal family of Aboussir. That's why your cousin Sadia was chosen. And before you make any more accusations let me re-iterate there was no force involved. I asked and she accepted.'

Miranda snorted. 'You might have chosen Sadia but she didn't choose you. As for asking her, what choice did she really have?'

Dark eyebrows shot high on that bronzed face. 'Your cousin is an adult and perfectly capable of saying no.'

He'd touched a nerve. Miranda would never have allowed herself to be railroaded into a marriage. But Sadia was completely cowed by her father.

'As if! With her father breathing down her neck? You've no idea how he's always bullied her and how little autonomy she has.'

His eyes widened and she thought she read shock, even dawning horror there. But the impression was gone before she could be sure. '*If* you're to be believed. For all I know you had your own motives for the kidnap. Jealousy, maybe, that *you* weren't chosen as a royal bride.' Miranda gasped, stunned at the notion. She itched to set him straight but knew it would be pointless. 'But you're nothing like your cousin.' He sneered. 'At twenty-three you're so confident that you've already embarked on a career of criminality and kidnap.'

Her mouth snapped shut, her conscience in flames. Until she processed everything he'd said. 'How do you know my age?'

'Hassan and his team brought phones. We've done a little research, confirming your identity among other things.'

She didn't know which she disliked more. The idea of them poking into her private life, or that Hassan had brought reinforcements. No doubt the place was surrounded, so any fragile hope of escaping grew more tenuous.

She drew a shuddering breath and shoved her hands behind her back, clasping them where he wouldn't see how they shook. 'Sadia is on her way here, then.'

'No. I've made other arrangements.'

Miranda sagged in relief.

Annoyingly, this man made it sound as if he had a bevy of willing women ready to marry him.

But then his wife would have riches, luxury and status. Some women would see a loveless marriage to a cold-hearted man as a small price to pay for all that. It would have destroyed Sadia, who'd already suffered at the hands of her dictatorial father.

'You've changed your mind about marrying into the royal family?'

Yet in that case, why keep her here to witness the event? Why not send her off to prison now?

He folded his arms, the movement emphasising the power in his tall frame. Miranda shivered again, remembering how it had felt to be pinned against him.

To her consternation, the memory wasn't wholly negative.

'I've already explained it's vital I marry into your Sheikh's family.'

Miranda scowled at him, mind racing as she mentally flicked through the leaves of the family tree. She didn't know all the distant relatives as well as she might because she'd spent so long overseas. How many unmarried females of marriageable age were there?

'It's not my bride coming here, it's the cleric who'll officiate at the wedding and a representative of her family to witness it.'

Revelation was a glare of searing light even as Miranda's vision darkened at the edges. Her breath rattled and she had to drag in more oxygen before attempting to speak.

He beat her to it. Gleaming eyes held hers. He didn't bother concealing his mockery.

'I see you finally understand. How fitting that my bride should be the woman who tried to steal my throne from me and destroy everything our governments have worked for. Who caused this mess in the first place.'

He leaned in so she inhaled that intriguing aroma of cedarwood and virile man.

'*You* will be my bride. We'll marry in an hour.'

CHAPTER FOUR

MIRANDA WANTED TO protest he couldn't mean it. It was impossible that they'd marry.

But the implacable light in those dark eyes spoke of sombre determination.

Even so she heard herself saying, 'I'm sorry. Really sorry about that glitch in your plans.'

Not for disrupting the marriage to Sadia but...

He stood so near she *felt* the vibration of his deep voice as a ripple through her belly. 'It's too late for apologies. The damage is done.' His nostrils flared as if he reined in impatience. 'You should have thought before you acted.'

Her shoulders hunched high at the familiar refrain.

Her uncle had spent years castigating her for being thoughtless, impulsive, a disappointment. Even when she tried to live up to family expectations, feigning interest in domestic skills that bored her to tears. Trying to hide her exuberance behind a prim façade that always cracked.

'But I didn't know about your coronation. I was just trying to save my cousin.' His jaw flexed on the word *save* and she hurried on. 'Surely there's another way—'

'If there were another way, I'd take it.' She felt the

waft of his breath on her face. He spoke slowly, branding every word deep. 'I wouldn't be in this ruin waiting for a makeshift wedding I don't want. And—' his stare skewered her '—I definitely wouldn't choose to marry someone like you.'

His venom was understandable, yet she winced inwardly at his lashing disapproval. She was stunned to discover that, far from wearing it as a badge of honour, she didn't like it.

Why should it matter what he thought of her?

Miranda had a lifetime's experience of disapproval and had learned to appear unmoved despite how that hurt.

Her foreign mother hadn't fitted into this country so her daughter had had little chance of being accepted. When Miranda's father had died young she'd spent years shuttling between visits to her mother, in whichever country she was working, and here. Miranda had never fitted anywhere, especially in conservative Aboussir. She'd never blended in.

Surely that was the key to her salvation now.

Instead of retreating, she stood her ground. As if dealing with a furious sheikh, who looked as if he'd rather toss her into a dungeon than marry her, were no more difficult than breaking in a spirited horse.

She must be woozy from stress and dehydration. For a moment her wayward brain actually wondered how Sheikh Zamir would respond if she stroked his lean cheek and whispered that he was a good boy, as if he were a highly strung stallion.

How would that square, bronzed jaw feel against her palm? Would the animosity in his eyes soften to something else?

Miranda ducked her head, biting her lip to hold back a bubble of hysterical laughter. And something that wasn't laughter. A sensation low in her body that made her want to shift restlessly and press her thighs together. She blinked and cleared her throat.

When she looked up again, his disapproving scowl had been replaced by a look that might almost hint at concern. It caught something high in her chest. For two whole seconds, as he surveyed her and she couldn't look away, heat crept along her chilled bones.

The feeling was so unfamiliar Miranda actually debated feigning illness. Anything to escape this situation and this man.

She'd never fainted in her life but if he believed her to be ill, he'd have to drop his farcical plan.

Or maybe whoever he brought in to officiate wouldn't care if the bride was comatose. This wasn't a normal marriage but a dynastic necessity.

Besides, Miranda wasn't that good an actor. More importantly, she had too much pride to pretend. Whatever happened, she wanted to be awake and aware.

'Of course you shouldn't marry someone like me. I'm totally inappropriate.' The words tumbled out so quickly she had to catch her breath. 'I'm rash and reckless. It would be a disaster if you married me.'

No one in their right mind would think her a suitable royal bride. Even she couldn't imagine it.

One expressive eyebrow climbed that broad forehead. 'True. But not as much of a disaster as if we don't.'

Miranda shook her head. 'You don't understand! I'd be a complete embarrassment. Even if I didn't mean to do the wrong thing, I would.' She saw no softening in his expression. 'Just look at me!' She gestured to her ill-fitting and now dusty uniform.

'Since you insist.'

With deliberate slowness his gaze travelled to her short, dishevelled hair, then down her body, not missing anything, before lazily rising again, igniting Catherine wheels of fire that twisted and flared under her skin.

Miranda had never experienced anything like it. She *knew* he'd done it to discomfort her and he'd succeeded. But his languid survey had been so thorough her flesh burned in mortification.

Not because there had been anything overtly sexual in that look. On the contrary, he might have been sizing up a horse he was considering acquiring, or a sports car, assessing whether it would meet his rigorous standards.

No doubt she failed those standards miserably. Not just because of the borrowed uniform. Her body compared unfavourably with the lush curves of her beautiful cousin. She'd never be the demure, self-effacing yet competent sort of woman that, according to her uncle, men sought in a wife.

But the horrifying fact remained that this man's slow perusal ignited sensations that were more than mortification. They felt like…arousal. Unwanted and inexplicable, especially given his obvious contempt.

She firmed her mouth and glared, hating the way he'd dragged old insecurities to the surface in such a short space of time then piled on new ones to torment her.

The man was dangerous.

'It's not an attractive outfit,' he murmured, 'but clothes are easily changed.'

Miranda scowled. Was he being deliberately obtuse?

'As for embarrassing me by doing the wrong thing…' He shook his head. 'No chance of that. I have no intention of letting you run amok without supervision. I've seen the damage you can do. You'll be closely monitored at all times.'

She swallowed, discovering her throat was tight and gritty. Anger and lack of water, she told herself. Not hurt.

After all, he just echoed what she'd said. What was obvious to anyone. Sooner or later Miranda always messed up and let people down.

Zamir watched her colour fluctuate and her eyes turn glassy. Just like a few moments ago when he'd felt an unaccustomed scrape at his conscience, as if he'd gone out of his way to hurt her.

He shifted his weight, not liking the feeling.

Was he being deliberately cruel?

This woman had all but destroyed every carefully laid plan not only for his marriage but his accession to the throne. And she'd done it with all the finesse of a shotgun blasting through flesh straight to his ego.

Beyond her obvious crimes, what really rankled was her appalled, dismissive tone when she'd spoken of his plan to marry her cousin. She'd acted as if he were some monster!

The notion left an unpleasant, metallic tang in his mouth.

Had Sadia really detested the idea of marrying him?

Never for one second had that occurred to him. Sadia had been sweet if quiet on the two occasions they'd briefly met. She'd shown no hint of reservations about their marriage.

Arranged matches had been the norm in royal families for generations. He'd assumed that she, like he, accepted the arrangement as a duty. The idea that she was so desperate to avoid their marriage she'd turned to her cousin in distress... Why hadn't she told *him*?

Despite the desperate urgency of today's events, that notion made Zamir feel wrong inside. He'd spent his life building himself into the man his people needed. Reliable. Decisive. Honourable.

Now this silver-eyed adventuress not only disrupted his plans but made him feel... Less.

Yet despite his justifiable annoyance, he didn't like the hurt he'd glimpsed in her either. But Miranda Fadel's feelings weren't his priority. He had a nation to think of. Two in fact.

He felt better when her chin tipped up again and her eyes narrowed. He preferred her argumentative to that suspicion of vulnerability.

'Even with the right clothes and the right minders, I wouldn't make a suitable wife.' Her voice was husky. With emotion, or was that her natural tone? Why did he even notice? 'I'm restless and impatient. I don't like sitting for long periods. I'd be no good at...' She waved one arm. 'Whatever royal wives do.'

'On the contrary, that energy will be useful. Being royal is rarely about sitting in one place for long.'

Zamir refused to let his thoughts stray to other directions where he could channel her restless energy. Yet he felt a stab of awareness in his tightening groin.

It was inexplicable. Miranda Fadel was a pest, a sow's ear that he'd have to turn into a silk purse and present to the public as a suitable wife. Because she'd left him no choice.

She was a thorn in his side and this spark of awareness must be the result of instant dislike. She was defiant and brash. She was Trouble with a capital T.

Yet he couldn't deny a piquant fascination at the
prospect of knowing her better.

His breath banked up in his lungs and the torsion in
his belly grew as he remembered her body against his,
breasts and hips and slender thighs moulding to his
harder frame. Her sweet breath against his throat and
the vibrant energy that seemed innate to her sparking
off something in him, reminding him that he was first
and foremost a man.

A man who'd been celibate too long while he shouldered the burdens of the sheikhdom as his uncle de-
clined.

'You don't understand.' Her eyes flashed and it
struck him that, for a woman who should be pleading
and persuasive, she was crackling with impatience. 'I
don't…' She shook her head. 'It's not just the clothes,
though I warn you I don't even own a dress. It's me.
I'm not…'

'Not what?'

Zamir was intrigued to find her lost for words. She
had no hesitancy spelling out *his* supposed flaws.

A knot formed in the centre of her forehead. 'I'm
not…' Her voice dropped. 'Feminine enough.'

Of all the objections she might have raised, that
hadn't occurred to him. Not feminine enough? Even
when she spat fury he couldn't help noticing the provocative, natural pout of her lush mouth. The way, when
she smiled, albeit sarcastically, her lips curved a little
downwards, and appeared all the more kissable.

Then there was the memory of her definitely feminine body against his.

'Women in my uncle's family are expected to blend
into the background. Not voice strong opinions or make
their own decisions. Not wear their hair short or work
in jeans. They're supposed to look and be—' she gestured vaguely with one hand '—sweet yet alluring, as
if butter wouldn't melt in their mouths.'

Zamir couldn't prevent his huff of amusement. The
notion of her sitting quietly, never voicing an opinion,
was too much.

To his amazement he saw a flash of hurt cross her
face. Did she think he couldn't imagine her as an alluring woman?

It seemed impossible. If she lost the pugnacity he
could readily imagine her cutting a swathe through any
men in her vicinity. Those stunning eyes alone were
mysteriously enticing.

Before he could respond, she continued. 'Then
there's the issue of my birth.'

'Pardon?' Zamir didn't recall anything about that,
but then his research into her background had been
necessarily brief.

'I could never be a king's consort.' She paused then
went on quickly. 'I'm what my uncle calls half-blood,
didn't you know? Only my father is from Aboussir.'

Zamir inhaled sharply. 'That's not a term I use, nor
anyone in my court.' He shook his head. 'Qu'sil is a
melting pot of people from many places. For centuries
it's been a crossroads for trade routes between east and
west, north and south.'

She stared back stonily, as if unconvinced. 'Perhaps
Qu'sil is different from Aboussir but I think it unlikely.'

Zamir was angered that her own family had considered her less because of her parentage. He felt his jaw firm.

'You're related through your father to a royal Sheikh. You're a member of his family.'

'But my mother was an American singer.'

He inclined his head. 'Whose own mother was Swedish. That's an asset, an instant link with the US, one of our key trading partners, and with a significant European country.'

She opened her mouth then closed it again, as if bereft of words. For a blessed few seconds, silence reigned.

He should have known it wouldn't last.

'You're twisting things. Trust me, you really don't want to do this. It would end in disaster and if you think the Sheikh of Aboussir would approve, you're wrong. He wouldn't want me representing the country. I'm the relative the family prefers not to mention.'

Zamir had heard enough. 'You're wasting your breath. This is happening as soon as the appropriate person arrives to officiate.'

He heard, as if conjured by his words, the distant throb of a chopper's rotors. Just in time.

'You created this mess, Ms Fadel, so you'll help resolve it. Don't look for a reprieve from me. I'm simply doing my duty and it's time you stepped up and did yours.'

Her face flushed and her eyes sparked. 'But you don't want me and I definitely don't want you!'

He'd have labelled her reaction childish, except there was nothing childlike about her. Even in that badly fitting uniform she was all vivacious woman. How had he, even for a moment, been taken in by her disguise?

The fact that his lack of attention had contributed to this appalling situation only added to his disgruntlement.

'You think I *wanted* to marry your cousin Sadia?' He paused, watching her eyes widen. 'This isn't about what I *want*, or about what *you* want. It's about what needs to happen for the sake of our countries. Therefore it *will* happen. And as for your Sheikh not approving of you as my bride...' He strode to the window to see the helicopter landing. 'Who do you think arranged for the cleric who has just arrived from the palace?'

Miranda's heart fluttered high against her throat. Her mouth dried. 'The Sheikh knows?' She waved both hands wide in a gesture that encompassed the musty room. 'He knows about this? About me and—'

'He does. And he agrees it's the only solution.' Sheikh Zamir looked down his imperious nose. 'I'm not the only one with a vested interest. He and my uncle instigated arrangements for the original marriage, and for the union of our nations.'

Miranda shook her head, trying to take it in. 'But surely he doesn't approve of me as a replacement for my cousin. As a representative of his family and our country.'

True, the Sheikh himself had never specifically voiced his disapproval of her, but her close relatives, particularly her uncle, had made it clear that she let the family down in multiple ways and was only accepted out of family loyalty.

'On the contrary, he thought it an excellent solution.

Which is why he's sent the appropriate people to ensure the wedding goes as it should.'

Miranda barely heard anything after his first few words. The idea of her stepping into the limelight as a royal bride was impossible!

But she heard the helicopter and knew he wasn't lying. He had the smug arrogance of a man about to get his own way.

The roar of the chopper melded with the roar of her thundering pulse and she shuffled her feet wider, trying to steady shaky limbs.

'No one will believe it. Royalty marries in front of a huge audience, not in the middle of nowhere.'

Dark eyebrows rose in a look of almost pitying superiority. 'Your cousin didn't tell you? I and my country are in mourning for my uncle so the ceremony was to be private. There will be time for a public celebration later, after the period of mourning is over and I'm crowned.' He paused, his gaze piercing. 'All we need today is the actual, legal ceremony.'

'Oh, if that's all then clearly there's no problem. Unless you count a forced bride!' Miranda's hands landed on her hips. 'You really think you have the right to do that? It's illegal. It's wrong. It's—'

'Happening.' His gaze pinioned her to the spot. When he spoke again his voice was silky with threat. 'I *will* marry today, and my bride *will* be from your family. There's no other option.'

As she looked into that unblinking gaze, Miranda's stomach dropped. She'd intended to refuse his outlandish scheme, no matter how he blustered. After growing up in her uncle's household she had no desire to put herself under the control of a powerful man.

Except she suddenly recalled one obvious fact that in her stress she'd overlooked. Sadia had a younger, unmarried sister. If Miranda refused to cooperate there was still time to fly Amal here before the Sheikh's midnight deadline.

All the fight bled out of Miranda. She couldn't save Sadia and then let Amal potentially take her place.

An inner voice protested that the Sheikh hadn't mentioned Amal. Surely he wouldn't stoop to that. But the truth was she didn't know him. She had no idea what he was capable of.

You're the one who created this situation. You'll have to be the one to step up.

'I despise you,' she whispered in a voice rough with anger.

Those gleaming eyes narrowed and his mouth tightened, but of course something as negligible as her hatred wouldn't sway him. If anything his hauteur only increased.

'You are entitled to your private opinions.'

'You surprise me. Are you sure you're not going to monitor those as well?'

His glare was formidable yet, unlike her uncle, he didn't let his fury leak out. That surprised her.

'As long as they're private, not expressed in public, you're free to believe what you wish.'

As if he had the ability to dictate her thoughts!

She seethed.

'You'd really marry a woman who can't stand you?' Miranda tilted her head, trying to discover what was going on behind that hard, handsome face. Then a thought struck her and dazzling hope rose, making her dizzy. 'But it won't matter, will it? Once all the fuss dies down and the two countries are joined we can quietly divorce.'

She hadn't even finished when he shook his head. 'No divorce. So if you're thinking of trying to get out of this by making a scandal, think again. Our union is a symbol of the union of our countries. Because of that you're needed by my side. You'll remain my wife.'

Miranda opened and closed her mouth but words wouldn't come. It had been her last hope. Even now, in the distance she heard muffled noises. The others had arrived.

This was real. They were going to marry.

It didn't feel real. Her vision blurred and she felt a curious, sweeping sensation in her stomach. Despite her locked knees, the floor seemed to ripple beneath her feet.

Large hands grasped her elbows and he was there, in her private space, towering above her. His eyes looked blacker than ever but instead of familiar disapproval she imagined a softer expression.

'You need to sit.'

She shook her head then regretted it when the world spun. He was right but she refused to acknowledge it. 'I need water. I haven't had anything to drink since I collected you from the hotel.'

'You what?' His voice rose. Funny, when she'd insulted him his voice had gone soft and lethal, not loud. 'Don't you know how dangerous it is to dehydrate in this climate?'

Miranda rolled her eyes as he sat her down into a chair. 'Duh! Of course I know. I was born here. But when we arrived I was concerned about you. I was getting water for you when you ambushed me and—'

'I understand.'

To her amazement she saw colour streak his chiselled cheekbones as if he were embarrassed. For not offering her water after she kidnapped him? It didn't seem possible. It wasn't as if she'd asked for a drink and he'd refused.

Miranda had the creeping suspicion that Sheikh Zamir was more complex than she thought.

'Don't move.' He crossed to the door in a few long strides. 'And don't think of trying to run away. You'd just embarrass yourself.'

He didn't stop to see her reaction but disappeared without a second glance. Naturally Miranda took the opportunity to push up out of the chair, only to fall back.

She told herself she was weak from dehydration. Stupid not to have drunk all day. But it was more than that. Stress, shock and the deep voices from just down the corridor made her, for once, give in. She slumped, defeated, knowing she didn't have the strength to escape.

Defeat was a rusty tang on her tongue.

It was only when his high and mightiness strode back into the room, bringing a tall glass of water and an air of crackling energy, that she straightened her spine and conjured the appearance of aloof disdain.

'Thank you.'

Miranda took the glass carefully so as not to touch his fingers, then drank thirstily, not deigning to meet his eyes. If she was going to be a queen she might as well borrow some of his arrogance. The thought brought a disbelieving laugh and she choked on a mouthful.

Her gallows humour vanished when he moved closer. 'I'm fine.'

She threw up her hand to ward him off, catching his

unreadable stare. Just as well. Who would want to get inside this man's thoughts?

'The cleric and witnesses are here. The marriage will take place in the largest sitting room.' His tone was so bland he might have been commenting on the latest stock market figures. Not their *marriage*. How could he be so unmoved by it? 'It's still a sumptuous room, despite the neglect. It will make a good background for the photo.'

'Photo? You're going to take a photo?'

'Just one. To show the happy bridal couple.'

Because it was important to him to share the news the marriage had taken place.

He frowned down at her as if seeing her properly for the first time. She was exhausted, no doubt washed out from stress and the unflattering beige uniform, her face bare of make-up, and not wearing a single item of jewellery. Even without a mirror, Miranda knew she looked nothing like a blushing bride.

She drained the glass then folded her arms. 'People will take one look at me and know there's something fishy about this marriage.'

Let him fix that! Her guess was that he'd arranged the legalities of this union but hadn't given a thought to her appearance.

She couldn't keep the sly satisfaction from her voice as she went on. 'Won't people think it odd that a prince should marry someone dressed as a chauffeur?'

For a second he surveyed her with what might, in another man, be dismay. Then he ordered, 'Undo your collar.'

He marched to a window and reached for a curtain

that, even dusty, was lustrous with the sheen of dark
blue silk, intricately embroidered with silver thread.

One powerful tug tore it free.

Miranda gasped. It was only a curtain, though an
heirloom piece made by hand generations ago. Yet his
abrupt, decisive action made her stomach clench.

Here was a man who leashed his emotions instead of
flaunting them but who didn't hesitate to act. He was
a man who made things happen. For some reason that
unsettled her.

He shook the fabric vigorously then turned. 'That
high collar's still done up.' He reached as if to rip it
open, when she quickly did it herself.

'I don't see what difference the collar makes.'

He frowned, presumably realising his attempt at a
makeover wouldn't work.

Then he reached out and flattened the fabric against
her collarbone. His touch was light yet she froze and
her breath grabbed high in her throat.

Eyes the colour of midnight filled her vision and for
an instant she felt...

He flung the heavy silk over her, draping her head
and settling it around her shoulders. Instinctively she
reached for it as he crossed it over her open collar and
breasts. Their fingers brushed and a curious sensation
started in her fingers and shot to her stomach.

Instantly he withdrew, his expression as severe as
carved stone. Clearly he hadn't felt that odd spark. To
him she was just a mannequin to parade in this farce.

'Come. It's time.' He stepped aside and held his hand
out. She looked down at his broad palm and remembered the feel of his body on hers.

She could have refused. She could have screamed

that this was the biggest mistake of their lives. But his steady look, and the knowledge that her reckless plan threatened to derail the well-being of their countries, stopped her.

She was responsible for that, however unwittingly.

Slowly Miranda rose.

Fifteen minutes later it was done. They were married. The agreement—she couldn't think of it as a ceremony—was witnessed by Zamir's aide, Hassan, the man she'd believed to be a bodyguard, and by her Sheikh's secretary, a distant cousin who'd regarded her with cool courtesy.

A single photo was taken of the bridal couple, Zamir looked regal and imposing in his white robe and she, wide-eyed and solemn but surprisingly bride-like, courtesy of the rich lapis-lazuli silk with its exquisite silver embroidery. And the richly engraved and surprisingly beautiful golden wedding band on her finger.

Moments later the photo was sent out publicly with a caption that referred to a quiet wedding in the presence of members from both the bride and groom's families.

It was done.

Miranda was married.

To a man she'd never seen before today. A man she'd kidnapped and who had every reason to hate her. A man determined that she should move to his country and play the part of his queen.

If it weren't so unthinkable it might be laughable.

She could only hope she woke tomorrow to discover it had been a bad dream.

CHAPTER FIVE

ZAMIR HADN'T SPENT much time thinking about his wedding night. He'd been too wrapped up finalising the arrangements between both countries and handling the plethora of tasks that fell to him on his uncle's death.

Not to mention wrestling his deep-seated grief for the man who'd raised him and his siblings after his parents died. Zamir had been just ten, Umar and Afifa five and three respectively, so their uncle had been the only parent the younger ones really remembered.

But even if Zamir had had time to think about his first night as a married man, he'd never have imagined this.

It was near midnight and, instead of being tucked up in bed with his wife, he was in a chopper, flying home with a prickly, infuriating troublemaker. The one with eyes that flashed bright as honed steel when she was angry. Or turned misty, dull and haunted when she was worried.

A steel band tightened around his gut as he remembered how she'd looked during the short, all-important ceremony.

She'd clutched the rich fabric to her in a white-knuckled hand and, for a defiant criminal, had looked remarkably fragile. Her eyes had been huge, making her seem younger than the mid-twenties he knew she was.

Yet she'd looked far more than young and scared.

With that drab uniform hidden by gleaming silk, she'd looked...stunning.

The revelation had hit like a blow.

He'd been too distracted to notice earlier, too busy scrabbling to avert the disaster she'd created to see her properly as a person, not an enemy.

To see her as a woman.

Her jaw was more angular than soft, but that only highlighted the sultry pout of her full-lipped mouth. *That mouth.* Her lips tilted down at the corners, creating apostrophe grooves in her cheeks when she was amused. They flashed like an invitation to share a private joke, undermining his impatience and making him want to lean down and taste her intriguing mix of obstinacy and disarming allure.

Zamir shifted restlessly, telling himself he was merely impatient to get home.

Yet he couldn't help surveying the woman beside him. Of course she wasn't asleep. She was too determined for that, staring into the night sky as if searching for trouble. He could almost hear the wheels racing in her brain as she assessed her new circumstances.

Was she aware of him watching her? Her shoulder lifted a fraction. Tension? An attempt to put a barrier between them?

Too late for that. They were husband and wife.

The reality slammed into him.

It was one thing to accept marriage to Sadia, the pleasant if quiet woman he'd met briefly.

He'd had no expectation, ever, of marrying for personal preference. A dynastic marriage had been inevitable, his duty to his position and his people.

But a hole-and-corner marriage to a meddling firebrand who was determined to be as difficult as possible…!

Zamir pinched the bridge of his nose, fighting the remnants of the migraine that still hadn't completely gone.

Her recklessness needed to be curbed. Boundaries set. Some sort of understanding reached. For, no matter their personal views on this marriage, it was real and they had to live with it.

Yet more things to add to his never-ending list of urgent tasks.

Zamir grimaced. He had a feeling everything else on that list, like amalgamating the laws and governments of two countries, would prove much simpler than transforming his bride into a suitable queen. He'd have to have her watched constantly and organise lessons on court customs, politics, deportment…no, not deportment. She already had the posture of an empress.

He slanted another look her way, lingering on her profile. She wasn't pretty like her cousin.

She was something more disturbing. His new bride was proud, innately graceful, and possessed a bone-deep elegance that he guessed would improve with age.

Zamir recalled the photo online of her stunning mother. His new wife had that same eye-catching allure, though she hid it beneath bad temper and aggression.

'It's rude to stare.'

She didn't even turn, just looked ahead towards the sprinkle of lights that marked the outskirts of Qu'sil's capital.

'I'm not staring. I'm taking stock.'

Slowly she turned and even in the dimly lit helicopter Zamir felt that distinct buzz of response as their eyes met. Earlier he'd put that down to annoyance. Now he wasn't so sure.

'Taking stock of your new acquisition?' Her top lip curled. 'I'm not a piece of livestock.'

No, she was something infinitely more problematic. *His wife.*

The rotor blades slowed as Zamir disembarked and walked around the helicopter. Hassan had already opened the door for his new queen, standing alert in case she needed assistance to alight. Instead she sat, unmoving, gaze fixed unblinkingly ahead.

Zamir looked from Hassan to his wife.

Wife! A phantom punch to the solar plexus accompanied the thought.

'You can go, Hassan, and see to that one matter for me. We'll debrief later.'

Hassan nodded, turning the movement into a bow for both Zamir and the unmoving figure in the chopper.

When Hassan's footsteps died away Zamir moved closer, holding out his hand. 'Come, it's time to go.'

She didn't move.

He squeezed his eyes shut for a moment, trying to conjure patience at the end of one of the longest, most difficult days he could recall. Given what she'd done to him it was tempting simply to upend her over one shoulder and carry her inside. He was tired, his head thumped and another sleepless night beckoned as he arranged to make their hasty marriage appear as a personal and political triumph.

But despite her accusation about him forcing her cousin, Zamir preferred persuasion to force. Besides, when he opened his eyes it was to see her swallow hard, her throat working, her mouth pressed tight.

It wasn't just stubbornness that motivated her.

She'd reaped what she'd sowed, interfering in things that didn't concern her and paying the price. But Zamir knew things weren't usually so black and white, even if in his fury earlier it had seemed that way.

He softened his voice. 'I promise I mean you no harm.'

That jerked her head around, her pale gaze meeting his with the force of a lightning bolt. What was that sensation? Pity at the distress she tried to hide or something else? Something that stirred a decidedly masculine awareness?

'It's been a long day and we both need rest. Things will look better in the morning.'

She gave a strangled huff of laughter. 'You think so?'

'I know so.'

His experience of traumatic events, the loss of his parents to a tragic accident while he was still a child, and the loss more recently of his uncle, had proved that embracing each new day was the only way forward.

'Then you're more optimistic than me.' Her voice had a quality that brushed across his skin. 'But you haven't just had your life and freedom stolen away.'

Zamir drew another calming breath. He wouldn't snap back at her jibe. Though his life, as much as hers, had now changed in unwanted ways.

'You make it sound like a fate worse than death. Many women would envy you. Becoming Queen of Qu'sil is a privilege, not a penance.'

Her dark eyebrows arched high. 'That's debatable, since it comes encumbered with marriage to you.'

So much for détente. The gloves were off now.

'Fine. If you feel that way, stay here.'

He looked at the pilot, still wearing his headphones in an effort to give them privacy, running through his post-flight routine. Zamir had had enough of her effrontery for one night. He stepped away.

'I'll let you explain to the staff who find you here in the morning who you are and why you chose to sleep here instead of in your own suite.'

'My own suite?'

Her whisper made him pause. 'Of course your own suite.'

Hadn't she realised that, no matter how unorthodox the circumstances of their wedding, she was now his wife? Where did she think she was going to sleep? In a broom cupboard?

No, you fool. In your bed. That's where she'd thought she'd have to sleep.

The realisation sliced through him like a sharpened blade. Suddenly her obstinacy in not leaving the chopper took on a whole new meaning.

She'd thought he expected her to spend the night with him...

Zamir's gut spasmed.

He had as many flaws as the next man, though he did his best to rise above them. But as far as he knew no one had ever regarded him as an ogre. Or sexual opportunist.

'A suite by myself?'

He drew himself up straight, meeting her eyes. 'Absolutely.' Then, because he *was* as human as the next man, he added, 'You'll have your privacy. And I'll spend what's left of tonight dealing with the fallout of today's events.'

If he'd thought to make her feel guilty or apologetic, he'd been wrong.

'In that case, I'll come with you.'

Zamir suppressed a reluctant smile. She had the hauteur of a born queen, as if she were doing *him* a favour.

Which he supposed she was. If she were found here in the morning he'd have had to find an explanation for the inexplicable.

She shuffled forward in her seat then rose. Of course she ignored his outstretched hand and climbed out by herself. But her legs crumpled when she stepped onto the tarmac.

Swifter than thought, he swooped down to catch her. Her breath hissed but for once she didn't spit venomous words. Exhaustion, stress, and he suspected the remnants of the dehydration he should have noticed earlier, took their toll for the second time today.

He could support her all the way from the helipad, across two courtyards and into the palace proper. Or he could make it easier on both of them.

He swept her up against his chest, a bundle of enveloping blue silk and accusing mist-grey eyes.

'*Don't* tell me you can walk by yourself when clearly you can't.' He strode towards the palace. 'This will be quicker, which means we'll be rid of each other sooner. Besides, this way anyone who happens to be awake won't see a stranger in blue silk over a pair of men's trousers and boots. If you pull that silk over your feet any observer will only notice *us*, the romantic bridal couple.'

Her silence was loud with unspoken objections, though she did twitch the swathe of fabric to cover her boots.

He sighed. 'Can't we call a truce for now and resume hostilities in the morning? I'm sure you'll find me just as obnoxious then.'

A tiny, reluctant smile curved her mouth and Zamir was surprised by a responding tug low in his body.

As if he enjoyed making her smile.

He must be punch-drunk with exhaustion.

'And you'll find me as bothersome as ever.' For the first time he heard true lightness in her humour rather than sarcasm.

'I'm bound to make decisions you don't like,' he added.

'And I'm sure to make a fuss about them.'

Zamir nodded and, despite everything he'd been through, felt his mouth curl in a tight smile. 'It's good to know where we stand.'

'Absolutely. I've had enough surprises for today.'

'*You've* had enough surprises?' He shifted his hold, carrying her more securely as he took a short flight of steps down into a courtyard filled with fragrant citrus blossom. 'You should try being kidnapped.'

Her huff of breath was a waft of warmth against his chin. 'Remarkable as it seems, since you've made it clear I should be prostrate with gratitude at the honour you've done me, *this* feels like kidnap.'

Zamir shook his head as he carried her through a marble portico. 'On the contrary, you had a choice. It was your actions that led to this situation. And it was you who finally chose marriage.'

He felt her sharply indrawn breath as much as heard it. 'I don't call that choice, I call that blackmail.'

'I call it doing what was necessary to save the future of both our countries.'

'Because no one other than you could possibly rule them,' she muttered, all trace of humour gone.

'They could,' he conceded, 'but I'm the one who's been trained to do it. I'm the one the people and the governments trust. The one who can make it happen without civil unrest or partisan squabbles. Long-term peace and stability are more important than our personal preferences.'

For once she didn't argue. But Zamir knew she was far from conceding the argument. She was tense in his arms as if ready to assert herself at any moment.

As before, it surprised him that a woman who had so much sheer destructive energy should be so light in his arms.

He told himself he was pleased she kept silent as they crossed into the second large courtyard. He was tired of argument, yet those fleeting moments of mutual understanding as they baited each other had felt surprisingly good. Almost like the banter he shared with his siblings.

Except with this woman there was an undercurrent lacking in dealings with his family. An undercurrent of awareness. Sexual awareness.

Finally they reached the side entrance to the palace and there was Hassan, waiting in the shadows.

'No complications?' Zamir asked.

Hassan shook his head. 'Everything is as you asked. There was a maid waiting to look after your bride but I told her she wasn't needed tonight.'

'Thanks.'

With a nod Zamir dismissed him and headed towards the royal apartments.

His bride shifted in his hold, making him all too aware of her soft curves against him. 'Why send the maid away? Because I'm such an embarrassment?'

He looked down into her set features. She was far too ready to take offence.

'Admittedly your clothes would make the staff curious. But the maid will see them in the morning when she clears them away. Don't worry,' he said when her expression changed to dismay. 'My staff are loyal and discreet, particularly those who work in the private apartments. There won't be gossip outside the palace about what you were wearing.'

Zamir turned a corner, approaching a familiar set of apartments. 'I asked Hassan to send her away because I thought *you* might be embarrassed, arriving in such an unconventional outfit.'

She stiffened and, looking down, he saw the unbelievable had happened. He'd managed to surprise this exasperating woman into silence.

CHAPTER SIX

MIRANDA'S SUITE WAS the size of a house. It contained a sitting room, dining room, study, media room, a walk-in wardrobe big enough to fit a three-seater sofa and copious hanging space, a hedonistic bathroom and the most romantic bedroom she'd ever seen. It combined decadent luxury with a pared-back elegance that made her breath catch.

Her stepfather, Matias, was wealthy but his sprawling Argentinian ranch house was nothing like this. Even the Sheikh's palace in Aboussir, which she'd visited, seemed fussy and outdated by comparison.

Miranda wanted to loathe it. Instead she was seduced by its comfort. The quiet. The unending hot water she used to try washing away her sense of unreality and fear. The lavish banquet laid out just for her that would have easily fed a family. She demolished half of it before tumbling into the cloud-soft bed.

A real queen would have pecked daintily at those delicacies. Whereas she, with her quick metabolism and active lifestyle, always needed plenty of fuel.

There were so many reasons she wasn't cut out to be royal. Why couldn't *he* understand that?

Her last thought before plunging into sleep was that Sheikh Zamir was the most infuriating, stubborn man on the planet.

For the first time in memory she woke late.

The sun was high, revealing she even had her own lap pool. Its green and gold mosaic tiles evoked the graceful leaves of a date palm. Swimming in that sparkling water would be like taking a dip in a private oasis.

Miranda resisted temptation. Who knew when Zamir would want to see her? She preferred to be fully clothed when they next met. She suspected it inevitable he'd compare her streamlined frame with Sadia's hourglass figure.

Usually Miranda didn't stress about her looks. She'd grown up in the shadow of a supremely beautiful mother and knew she wasn't in that league. Looks were irrelevant in her daily life.

Yet the idea of Zamir, with his austere charisma and his superiority, viewing her as second best compared with the bride he should have had—she didn't want to go there.

Muffled sounds drew her attention and she grabbed the ivory wrap that matched the lacy nightdress she'd worn last night.

Did Zamir have a store of sexy night things for visiting lovers?

She'd been loath to wear the seductive nightdress but had given in, preferring not to be naked. Using that grimy uniform again wasn't an option.

She refused to meet him in her bedroom. Tying the robe securely, she entered the sitting room.

'Madam. Good morning.' A woman in a tailored suit curtsied.

Curtsied! Any lingering hope Miranda had that last night had been some strange dream shattered.

Of course it was no dream. She was in Zamir's palace, wearing the exquisitely engraved, antique gold ring he'd produced at their wedding and slipped on her finger.

The ring he'd planned to give her cousin. But which, in a twist of mocking fate, fitted Miranda perfectly.

The ring she'd meant to remove last night then forgotten.

She put her hand to her throat, trying to still her racing pulse. 'Good morning. And you are?'

The head of housekeeping, it transpired. Here with Qu'sil's top fashion designer and an initial selection of garments. 'Just until your bespoke wardrobe is created.'

Bemused, Miranda stared at the women uncovering wheeled racks of clothes and trolleys piled with boxes. The sight was daunting for a woman who lived her life in jeans or jodhpurs.

Shopping had never been her favourite thing. Miranda had too many memories of her mother finding fault with what she chose then throwing up her hands in despair when the clothes she persuaded Miranda to try didn't suit her.

The housekeeper chivvied her staff. 'Quickly now. Madam has an appointment at midday.'

'Appointment?' Dread settled in her stomach. She knew nothing about being a royal. Sheikh Zamir couldn't expect her to appear in public!

The woman nodded. 'The Sheikh is expecting you.'

Miranda's mouth set mutinously. She had no intention of dancing to his tune.

But there's no point avoiding him. There are things you need to discuss.

Didn't anyone else think it strange that Zamir should make an *appointment* to see his wife on the day after their wedding? But then everyone knew this wasn't a love match but a marriage of convenience.

Inconvenience, more like.

Swallowing her pride, she admitted, 'It would be good to have something suitable to wear.'

Another woman stepped forward, introducing herself as the designer.

'It's a great honour to dress you, madam. And it's such a welcome gesture.' At Miranda's querying look she went on. 'Choosing a new wardrobe designed and made in your new country.' Her smile was warm. 'That decision will be much appreciated here.'

That was the story Zamir was using to explain her need for clothes?

'I'm glad you think so.'

'Oh, it is. There's been a lot of investment in local industry lately but in fields like engineering and robotics. Not fashion or textile production. This will bring welcome interest to our work.'

Not much riding on her appearance, then. Only the hopes of an eager industry.

Miranda stiffened. She suspected she was going to be a disappointment. She knew nothing about fashion.

'I hope I do you proud.'

The designer surveyed her with a practised eye, as Miranda might assess a new horse. 'There's no doubt about that, especially given the way you carry yourself.'

Her posture? The last time she'd thought about that was as a child learning to ride, being told to sit up and keep her shoulders back.

'Now, if I may?' The woman clicked her fingers and a horde of helpers encircled Miranda.

Miranda strode up the wide corridor, thankful the directions to the Sheikh's office were simple.

On the way she nodded to staff who bowed or curtsied. That made her feel like a fraud. She didn't feel royal.

She was a pretender about to be caught out.

No, that was yesterday. Masquerading as a driver. Caught in an abduction. Creating an international incident.

And paying the price.

Still it didn't seem believable. Even wearing this bejewelled tunic of silk so soft it fluttered against her like the touch of butterfly wings. And silver-grey trousers of equally fine silk.

Clothes fit for a queen.

Miranda had seen herself in the mirror and for a second hadn't known herself. She looked so...put together. Glamorous even. The chartreuse green was a colour she'd never worn. The style comfortable yet chic. The stylist had insisted she ditch the stud earrings she always wore and by that stage Miranda had given up objecting. Her new earrings of matching beaded silk and silver looked like delicate, hanging lilies and made her neck seem long and graceful.

Or maybe she just wasn't used to seeing herself in something other than jeans and a work shirt. When she'd insisted on wearing trousers, seeking confidence in familiarity, she'd had no idea she could look like *this*.

She even wore make-up, so light it was almost invisible, but enough to make her eyes look larger and her jaw softer.

Miranda didn't want to be soft. Her weakness yesterday horrified her, even if it had been from dehydration and shock. Today Zamir would discover she was no pushover.

She rapped on the last door and, without waiting for a response, opened it.

'Miranda. Come in.'

It was the first time he'd used her name and it stopped her on the threshold. *Not* because that deep voice sent heat coiling through her middle. That was nerves, or maybe residual anger.

She just hadn't expected him to use her first name. It seemed too intimate for what they shared.

Mutual distrust. Anger. Annoyance. Regret.

And a sizzle of something that felt like electricity building before a thunderstorm.

He sat behind a desk with a neat pile of papers in one corner, a massive computer screen and an old-fashioned blotter on which rested a large parchment. The edges of the parchment were decorated with intricate calligraphy and as she watched, he used a gold pen to sign it with a flourish.

He screwed on the cap of the pen and dropped it, eyes holding hers.

Impossibly, he looked even more arresting than he had last night. So much for hoping stress had exaggerated that.

But Miranda lived and worked in a man's world. She

wasn't easily intimidated, either by good-looking polo players who thought they were God's gift to women or by old-fashioned misogynists unused to women working in professional stables.

She pushed the door closed behind her and walked into the room, noticing how his eyes seemed to grow even darker as he watched her.

Was it the unfamiliar heeled sandals that made her hips sway? Or did she deliberately sashay? All she knew was that this wasn't her usual gait.

And the way Zamir surveyed her was unlike the way he'd looked at her yesterday.

Good. The sooner he realised she wasn't going to be meekly browbeaten, the better.

She reached the desk. 'Nice suit,' she murmured to fill the silence.

Not as nice as the body it covered.

Miranda blinked at the unwanted awareness thrumming through her.

So she liked wide, straight shoulders and strong arms. So what? A good body and a suave, bespoke suit weren't as important as a man's character.

'Thank you.' His mouth ticked up at one corner, making that sombre face far too attractive. 'Nice outfit. *Very* nice.'

He didn't ogle. She would have slapped him if he did. But his gaze holding hers ignited heat inside.

She shrugged, aware of the brush of thin silk and, even more, of her new lace underwear.

Maybe that was why she'd strutted into the room. She'd never worn anything against her skin that made her feel so innately feminine. Years living in her mother's shadow had made her defiantly uninterested in sexy lingerie. Instead of taking after her mother and becoming obsessed with her looks and clothes, Miranda had gone the other way, telling herself they didn't matter.

Yet suddenly she was glad for this morning's makeover. She felt not just feminine but assured in a way that was unfamiliar and which she liked very much. Especially when she saw Zamir's Adam's apple jerk.

'You wanted to see me?' She leaned in, resting hands on his desk, tilting her head so one dangling earring brushed her shoulder. Instantly she straightened. She was *not* trying to look coquettish.

'Yes. Take a seat.'

Miranda looked from the empty chair before his imposing desk to the seating area across the room. No way was she going to sit here being lectured like a pupil before a headmaster.

'Thanks, I will.'

Sauntering across the room, she chose an armchair with a view to the coastal city and the deep blue sea.

She took her time studying the collection of traditional ochre-coloured buildings and the cluster of highrises, some of them clearly works of art.

All the while she waited for his explosion of temper.

Her eyes widened when he strode into her line of sight and dropped into a nearby chair. Partly because *he'd* come to *her*. Partly because that charcoal suit outlined what yesterday's robe had hidden. That the man had the powerful thighs of a horseman. He shifted in his seat and the fabric stretched over flexing muscles.

Miranda's mouth dried.

She couldn't understand it. She was around athletic men all the time. Matias's friends and clients were professional athletes and none affected her like this. She lifted her hand to her forehead, checking for a fever on the pretext of brushing a stray hair off her face.

'You slept well? The accommodation was comfortable?'

'I did, and it is, thank you.'

But I'm ready to go home. I want to end this charade.

Yet she wasn't so naïve. There was no easy way out. If there had been he'd have already taken it.

'How long do we have to do this?'

He frowned. 'Talk?'

'Stay married.'

Horizontal lines grooved his brow, but even scowling the man looked good. Yet another annoying thing about him.

'I told you there can be no divorce.'

Her voice rose a notch. 'But you were just saying that to scare me.'

'I'm not into empty threats. I told you the truth. This marriage is permanent. It has to be.'

And just like that her hope bled away, because Zamir looked as happy about it as she was. Which was not at all.

But Miranda never gave up easily. According to her uncle it was one of her besetting sins. 'Surely, after the fuss dies down, when everything is sorted—'

'We'll stay together. Our union is a vital part of our countries' amalgamation. A symbol.'

'I don't care about symbols. I care about my freedom. Look.' She leaned forward, spreading her hands palm up. 'I'm willing to go along with this for a while. It's a mistake thinking I can play the role of queen long term, but I'll do my bit while the amalgamation happens. A few months.' His expression remained stony. 'A year, max. I know I owe you because of the abduction. It was a desperate thing to do and it had unintended consequences and I'm truly sorry.'

'I'm sorry too. This isn't what either of us planned but we're here now and we'll make the best of it.'

She sat back, stung by his stony-faced rejection. She felt the blood drain from her face, panic plunging like a lead weight in her abdomen.

'Then I won't bother with your cooperation. I'll file for divorce myself.'

'Unfortunately that's impossible.' He raised his hand to stop her words. 'The law forbids it.'

'You have no divorce here?' She didn't believe it.

'We do, but not in the royal family. Royal marriages are arranged for reasons of state. All parties need to be sure there will be no turning back at a later date. There *can* be no divorce.'

Miranda's eyes bulged. 'You really mean it! We're trapped?'

'We are.'

Oh, Miranda, what have you got yourself into?

It was one thing to help Sadia escape an unwanted match. But to trap herself permanently...

She shivered and wrapped her arms around herself. It couldn't be true. It couldn't. Yet why would he lie about something she could check?

'So it's a life sentence.' Her tone was flat.

There'd be no assistance from her family or her distant relation the Sheikh of Aboussir, who'd given his approval. And Matias, while wealthy, didn't have the influence to free her from this.

'You're determined to make the worst of this, aren't

you?' Zamir's frown was thunderous. 'Being my queen is a privilege, not a penance.'

'You said that last night but I'm not convinced.' She flicked her finger against her earring. 'Despite the charming fripperies that come with the position.'

Something shifted in his expression. Something that, for a fleeting moment, almost looked like amusement.

That yanked her from self-pity to outrage. She lunged forward in her chair, invading his space. She refused to be the butt of his amusement. 'This isn't a laughing matter.'

'For once we're in agreement. This situation will be catastrophic if we don't manage it properly.' He leaned forward too, so close she saw tiny flecks of light in his inky eyes. His warm breath feathered her as he spoke. 'For the record, any humour was self-directed. I've never in my life met a woman so determined to be unimpressed by me or my status.'

He shook his head slowly, holding her stare, and Miranda had the disquieting feeling that she couldn't pull back even if she wanted to, which, strangely, she didn't.

'It occurs to me, Miranda, that you'll be excellent for keeping my ego in check. If you don't drive me crazy in the process.'

His mouth quirked at the corner. It wasn't a smile, just the merest shadow of a hint of one. And it did something weird to her. Not just that fluttery feeling in her throat. It actually *did* lighten the pall of despair.

Like last night when, for a few precious minutes, they'd exchanged banter like equals. It had felt almost like camaraderie and made her wonder if buried behind the formidable authority and self-assurance was a man she could relate to.

You're seeing what you want to see because it's better than facing reality.

'Gratifying as the knowledge is, it's not the summit of my ambitions to keep your ego in check, or even to make your life difficult. There are other things I want from life.'

'Like what? Tell me, Miranda.'

She shook her head and made to sit back. Except a large hand covered hers and she stilled. She could easily have shaken off his touch. He barely gripped her, yet the sensation of skin on skin and the curiosity in those velvety eyes stopped her.

'Nothing glamorous or high profile. It's much more mundane.'

Zamir inclined his head. 'My role is high profile but most of the glamour is on the surface. It's hard work learning to be leader of a country. A lot of it's mundane, work behind the scenes that few ever know about.'

There it was again, that momentary feeling of connection. Of course it was nonsense. But what could it hurt to tell him? They were stuck with each other for now.

'I'm a horse trainer. I work mainly for my stepfather, Matias Garcia, in Argentina.'

'I've heard of him. He was a top polo player.'

Miranda nodded. 'He's still a phenomenal player but now he concentrates on the breeding side of the business.'

'And you help him?'

She could read no nuance in his tone but was used to people assuming her job was a sinecure while she lived off her stepfather's money.

She sat back so Zamir's hand fell away.

'I work with his animals but with others too.' As well as running initiatives aimed at changing and enhancing peoples' lives through riding and caring for animals.

'You must be very successful to work in such a renowned stable.' Her eyebrows rose at Zamir's comment and he shrugged. 'We're very proud of our horses. Polo has been played here for longer than anyone can remember. I really do know of your stepfather.'

That wasn't what had surprised her. It was Zamir accepting her work as valuable. Or was he saying that to soothe her?

Yet it was better than the casual dismissal she got from some people who believed a 'mere slip of a woman' was out of place in a top-notch stable.

'There are stables here. Excellent ones. Not just for myself but for the mounted ceremonial guard.' Miranda sat straighter, interest piqued. 'You're welcome to ride any time.'

'But not to work.'

Zamir's eyes narrowed. 'I doubt you'll have time to work once your royal duties begin.'

Miranda bit back a protest that she wasn't interested in royal duties. He knew that.

'And when will that be?'

'You'll have a full schedule from now on. It's imperative you learn about our country, customs and ceremonies.' He looked away. 'But you won't go out in public yet. The Queen never appears soon after the wedding.'

That dark gaze returned as his words sank in and heat blistered under her skin.

'You mean—' she cleared her throat, self-conscious but needing to know '—because I'm expected to be exhausted from sharing your bed?'

The trouble was, looking at Zamir, the picture of virility, Miranda found that too easy to believe.

Those wide shoulders lifted. 'Dynastic marriages are about securing the future.' By him getting her pregnant with an heir. 'It's an ancient tradition that should probably change. But it plays into our hands. It means we have time to mould you, ready to face public scrutiny.'

Miranda shot to her feet and across the room. 'I have no interest in being moulded.'

'Bad choice of words. Forgive me. It will give you time to learn about this place and your role so you don't feel daunted or threatened.'

Oh, he was good. Too good. He made this sound as if it were for her benefit, not his.

Yet she saw it made sense. She already felt a complete fraud. How much worse if she didn't understand what was happening around her?

Miranda swung around, clasping her hands behind her back and planting her feet wide. 'We need to get something straight. I have no intention, ever, of sharing your bed, much less bearing your child.'

A shiver started at her nape, tracked down her spine and burrowed down through her middle.

Zamir said nothing for the longest time. Nor could she read his expression.

'Time will tell. We both have sexual needs.'

His bluntness, the way he explicitly yoked their needs together, dried her mouth. Did he *know* about those tiny, forbidden thrills of awareness she suffered around him? The idea was humiliating.

'But,' he carried on before she could protest, 'let me clarify that I'd never force you.' His jaw hardened like honed steel. 'Sex without consent is despicable.'

She breathed out, relieved. Yet her tension remained. Because he'd agreed so easily and she couldn't trust him? Because of his annoyingly offhand 'time will tell' as if she didn't know her own mind?

Or because perversely she'd be happier if he wanted *her*, not just out of convenience but because he couldn't resist her? Because, after a lifetime of being a misfit, she still hated the feeling that she wasn't good enough?

Where had that come from? It was asking for trouble and she already had enough of that. This situation was already dire. She didn't need the complication of him desiring her.

Or of desiring him.

'You really think you're so irresistible I'll end up begging to share your bed?'

Miranda whipped up her scorn but beneath it felt an undermining shiver of fascination at the images the words conjured.

His expression didn't change but she'd swear there was a spark of something in those piercing eyes that matched her own unsettled roil of physical awareness.

'You're doing an excellent job of resisting my fatal charm so far.'

His tone was wryly amused, just short of smug, as if that were exactly what he thought. Miranda's hackles rose but she bit off the argument rising to her lips.

'For now,' he continued smoothly, 'let's concentrate on getting through the next few weeks. And I have a demand of my own.' He rose and paced towards her. Pride dictated she hold her ground, though her shoulders inched high as he neared. 'That you behave, or try to behave, as befits a queen. No deliberate sabotage.'

Reluctantly Miranda nodded. Despite her reluctance she *did* understand how delicate this situation was. There was nothing to be gained by trying to cause a scandal. All she wanted was her freedom. 'Okay.'

'Good.' He thrust out his hand. 'Here's to the beginning of trust between us.'

Trust? It would be a long time before he earned that. But she had a vested interest in not antagonising the man who held all the power here. Miranda reached out and felt his fingers close around hers. It was like connecting with an electrical charge. Energy fizzed through her palm and up her arm, making the fine hairs on her body stand to attention and her nipples tighten.

She made to break contact but his fingers firmed. 'One last thing, Miranda.' He leaned closer. 'Given your penchant for reckless acts, don't even think about trying to run away. You'd be stopped in short order and I'd rather save you embarrassment.'

Her breath seized, filling tight lungs.

Save himself trouble, more like.

Her chin tipped high. 'Am I to have gaolers, then?'

He rubbed his thumb over the ball of her hand, sending a cascade of sparks across her skin. How did he do that?

'No gaolers. But as my queen you'll have an escort when you go out. Bodyguards and, for official events, advisers or attendants.'

Gaolers, in other words.

Indignation flared. He was taking away her freedom.

It's already gone. The moment you agreed to marry, you put yourself utterly in his power.

For a second she felt overwhelmed and that scared her. Usually she was good at looking ahead, rising above barriers put in her way. But not today, not with this man.

It felt disturbingly as if he already knew her too well and anticipated her every move.

Nonsense. That was tiredness talking.

Miranda tugged her hand free and ostentatiously wiped her palm down her trousers, disappointment bitter on her tongue. 'So much for trust.'

She pivoted on her heel and marched out of the door.

CHAPTER SEVEN

'So, what's she like, my mysterious new sister-in-law?'

Zamir pushed his chair back from the desk and scraped his fingers across his scalp as he shifted his grip on the phone.

He should have known Afifa would be full of questions. Umar might be the documentary maker in the family with a nose for a story, but their little sister could be guaranteed to probe when Zamir least wanted.

'Not mysterious. I told you, she's from the Aboussi royal family but she's been living elsewhere.' He knew some of her background but there was more to learn. Another priority.

'Elsewhere?' Afifa asked.

'Argentina for the last few years but before that sharing her time between Aboussir and the USA, Canada and the UK.'

Was that why she was so different to her cousin? Where Sadia was quiet and placid, Miranda was feisty, reckless, occasionally aggressive, and disturbingly vulnerable.

Disturbing because those glimpses into her softer side played on his guilt at how he'd herded her into marriage.

*Herded her? When she'd kidnapped him! And almost
destroyed the diplomatic solution their countries had
spent years planning.*

Her audacity rankled, as did the fact he'd been easy
prey to her scheme. No man appreciated such a blow
to his pride.

Yet despite that, his curiosity stirred.

What had Miranda's life been like? Her Aboussi
family wasn't concerned about her well-being after the
hasty wedding, just about limiting any stain on their
good name.

Absurdly, Zamir had felt indignant on her behalf.
If anyone had tried to coerce Afifa in that way, he and
Umar would have moved heaven and earth to protect
her.

He grimaced at the sour tang of remorse on his
tongue.

No wonder Miranda viewed him as a villain. But he
couldn't regret what he'd done. His people needed the
long-term peace and prosperity that would come from
joining the two kingdoms. What was one woman compared with that?

Even so, his conscience scraped at the memory of
her expression when she'd capitulated and agreed to
marry him. He'd been relieved when Miranda had finally acknowledged *she* was responsible to fix the crisis
she'd created. Yet that had been mingled with distaste
at needing to force her hand.

'She sounds interesting. But she's not the woman
you'd planned to marry. This one's Miranda, not Sadia.
What's the story, Zamir?'

'No story.' Not that he was ready to tell his little sister. 'Just a change of plan.'

Her laugh sounded rueful. 'You do that stonewalling tone so well now, Zamir. Just like our uncle. Have you perfected the glare he used when someone annoyed him? You know, head up and nostrils flared, eyes narrowed. His don't-bother-me-or-you'll-be-sorry look.'

Zamir stiffened, realising that his nostrils *were* flared and his chin up. He frowned.

'You make him sound like a bully.' His uncle had taken on three orphaned children and loved them like his own.

'We both know he wasn't.' Afifa's voice softened. 'He was special. But you know what I mean. He was charming and caring but occasionally, if someone abused his trust, he went into that superior royal Sheikh mode.'

'He was imposing,' Zamir amended. 'And proud. A sheikh has to have presence.'

'I know. But he has to be approachable too. As he got older and sicker Uncle became more impatient, which made him seem daunting. I'd hate to think that had rubbed off.'

Zamir was about to protest that their uncle had devoted the latter part of his life to the taxing negotiations that would bring Qu'sil and Aboussir together. That his final thoughts had been for the well-being of his people. But it was true that in his later years, especially when in pain, his generous nature had often been concealed behind a stern persona.

'What are you saying, Afifa? That I'm becoming an autocrat? I haven't even officially taken the throne yet!'

'Of course not. You've never been hungry for power. You take duty too seriously for that. But you've got that same drive to do what you believe is right, no matter what. I just hope you don't seem too overpowering.' Afifa paused. 'This change of bride happened quickly. She's not too overwhelmed, is she?'

A huff of laughter escaped as he remembered Miranda several hours ago, leaning across his desk, skewering him with a condescending glare.

She *should* be overwhelmed!

Instead Miranda was confident, challenging and incredibly sexy. From the moment she'd sauntered into his office, all lithe femininity and vibrant sensuality, he'd had trouble keeping the thread of his thoughts. Even his anger had dimmed. He'd found it hard to keep his eyes on her face not her body. She had a combination of flagrant femininity, raw energy and not quite understated sexuality that yanked his libido into full awareness.

He'd already become acquainted with her body. Those memories were vivid. But seeing her in clothes that tantalised with glimpses of her delicious shape had knocked the air from his lungs and left him groping for control.

'Zamir? You didn't answer me.'

'Overwhelmed?' he scoffed. 'Not likely. It would take a lot more to knock Miranda's confidence.'

Like being carried off to a new country where she knew no one.

Like being thrust into a role she didn't know and didn't want.

Like being married to a stranger.

Knowing that stranger had power over her freedom, her life.

Zamir's amusement ebbed. He couldn't forgive her actions but his resentment was tempered by the knowledge she suffered for it now.

'I like the sound of her already. You need someone strong to stand up to you. I only hope she has a sense of humour too.'

He got to his feet and walked to the window, taking in the view of the city, reminding himself he'd acted for the good of his people. He'd had the best motives.

Who had said the road to hell was paved with good intentions?

'She does have a sense of humour.'

He recalled those moments of banter last night when they'd shared dark amusement over their situation.

At the time he'd been reassured, telling himself the situation wasn't too dire if they could laugh over it. He'd enjoyed Miranda's wry humour, feeling they briefly shared an understanding. Since his uncle had become ill and Zamir had taken on more of his role, there were fewer people with whom he could truly relax.

'I'm glad. You need someone to remind you to unwind and since Umar and I are on different continents…'

'How's the study going?'

'Good, thanks. Don't try changing the subject. I'll be back for the coronation so I'll see for myself how things are then. But meanwhile, Zamir, this marriage. Will it be okay? Will *you* be okay?'

It was on the tip of his tongue to say *he* wasn't the one she needed to worry about, but he wasn't that foolish.

'I know you swallowed Uncle's view that an arranged marriage is best for a royal.'

Her voice softened and Zamir knew she was thinking of their parents. Though Afifa didn't really remember them, her belief that they'd been devoted to each other had comforted her when they died and had somehow grown stronger over the years. He and Umar had never contradicted her.

She'd already made him promise not to arrange a suitor for her.

'I want you to be happy, Zamir. I want you to be with someone who will appreciate you.'

Zamir remembered the way Miranda had looked at him as if he were something filthy, discovered on the bottom of her shoe. Because he'd told the truth, that as his wife she would have aides and security staff whenever she went out.

He knew women who'd delight in that proof of their importance.

Trust him to find a spouse who hated the idea.

'You know I married because it was necessary.'

The words spilled into silence that felt stark with regret. Afifa's regret. But her heart was in the right place. She cared for him, the big brother who'd been there through the years of nightmares and distress after their parents' deaths, and later through the growing-up years. He'd always provided a shoulder to cry on, a listening ear, or been a coach, telling her to get up and try again when she failed at something.

'But despite that,' he heard himself say, 'Miranda isn't just a convenient bride.'

'You *like* her?' Afifa sounded eager. 'Really like her?'

Zamir hesitated, caught between the need to reassure and innate truthfulness. It was as he pondered that, he realised there were aspects of Miranda's character he did like.

And her body. Don't forget her body.

Scrubbing his hand across his face, he tried to corral his thoughts. 'She's challenging and opinionated—'

'She sounds perfect for you. If you married a pushover you'd be unhappy. And she's lovely. Don't forget I've seen the wedding photo, though she looked more startled than ecstatic.' He heard excitement in his sister's voice. 'But go on. Tell me, what else?'

'She's brave.'

Her courage, proven in that outlandish abduction, had been misplaced and inconvenient. But mettle was a good thing in a royal and certainly better than weak compliance. A loyal, courageous woman at his side—and Miranda was clearly loyal as shown by the lengths she'd gone to for her cousin—was exactly what he needed.

The knowledge was like a light flicking on in his brain.

'I...admire her,' he admitted finally.

It seemed he'd said the right thing. Afifa began chattering nineteen to the dozen, obviously believing it was only a matter of time before this marriage turned into a grand love affair.

The thought tugged Zamir's mouth into a rueful smile.

For that to happen he'd first have to overcome his wife's disgust. He suspected that if she heard he'd died in an accident, she'd have trouble repressing her glee. It was a good thing the old displays of weaponry had been taken down and moved to a museum when the palace was extended. He didn't fancy his chances if Miranda had access to a sword.

'So how are you wooing her?'

'Pardon?'

'Wooing her! Courting her. Getting her to fall for you.'

He only just stopped himself saying he wouldn't ask for the impossible, when Afifa went on. 'You're strangers but you've committed to spend your lives together. You need to get to know each other. Discover what she likes, make her happy, help her adjust to life in Qu'sil and with you. What are you doing to build on your relationship?'

First he'd have to *begin* a relationship. But out of the mouths of little sisters...

He had to smash the barriers Miranda insisted on erecting between them. For his country's sake, and his own.

'Actually, Afifa, that's something I want to work on this afternoon. It's been great talking but I need to go.'

'You're not going to tell me any more?'

'Not now. Anyway, it's time you got back to work. Watch out for those numbats.'

'You mean wombats. Numbats are in Western Australia not the east and—'

'Bye, Afifa. I really have to go.'

'Bye, Zamir. And good luck.'

He'd need it.

But for the first time today he had a glimmer of an idea how to go forward with this marriage.

He'd spent last night and today putting out potential spot fires caused by his radical change of wedding plans. It was crucial no one suspected their marriage was anything but amicable, stable and successful. Too much hinged on it as a first step to the much-awaited joining of their countries. He couldn't afford to let that fall apart when so many had given up so much to achieve union. His uncle had given his last, failing years to make this happen. Zamir *had* to see this through.

Yet since Miranda's visit to his study he'd been distracted. Not just by the conflicting feelings she'd elicited but by his body's response.

He'd wanted to reach for her, discover if the aura of sparking energy was real or imagined. And when he had, it had merely confirmed what he'd feared.

He wanted her. Badly.

Zamir had told himself the sexual desire between them was good, even if on her part it seemed more like a spark of hatred. Though the way her gaze had clung to his body told him there was more to her passion than dislike.

Nights of frantic work, that dying buzz of a killer migraine, not to mention kidnap and near disaster, had left him below par. Now, thanks to his sister, his thoughts cleared.

It wasn't enough to smooth the way for Miranda as his queen. To have her learn his country's customs and court etiquette. Or to have a suitable wardrobe. He needed to persuade her into accepting this marriage. Accepting *him*.

Persuade or seduce?

He grimaced. That was his ego talking. The ego she'd dented when she'd declared that nothing would persuade her to share his bed.

He'd told himself that was the least of the issues facing them. But statesman though he might be, he was also a man.

There'd be enormous satisfaction in having Miranda eat her words about never sharing his bed.

Who was he kidding? It wasn't words he cared about.

It was *her*. That frustrating, tempting bundle of contradictions that was his wife. The sexy woman with the luscious pout and enticing body.

Zamir had no intention of remaining celibate for the rest of his life. Nor was infidelity an option. But for now that could wait. His focus had to be overcoming her negative opinion.

He'd planned to give her time alone to adapt. But after speaking with Afifa he revised that.

Zamir returned to his desk. It was time to make a proper plan.

Miranda had assumed, after walking out on him earlier in the day, that Zamir would be too annoyed to spend time in her company. He was a proud, powerful man. She guessed he wasn't used to being crossed and what she'd done to him had been unforgivable. She understood his fury at being kidnapped. It was how she felt now. And since then, she hadn't pulled her punches, telling him exactly what she thought of him.

But Zamir surprised her. Mere hours after stalking out of his office she'd received a message inviting her to dine with him.

Inviting, not commanding. If it had been an order she wouldn't have obeyed. But an invitation…

That had sparked her curiosity so she'd arrived at the dining room to discover a table set for two and Zamir waiting for her, courteous, calm, the perfect host.

Any thought of resuming their earlier argument vanished when a group of musicians arrived and took up places on the far side of the room.

'Traditional musicians from the mountains of Qu'sil,'

Zamir explained. 'I thought you might like to learn a little more about our country while we eat.'

His smile had been charming and her hackles had risen defensively. But logically she had nothing to complain about.

They'd spent the evening as polite strangers, discussing general topics rather than the ones burning for resolution. Gradually she found herself enjoying the music, the food and even, occasionally, Zamir's insights.

The next evening was the same. Except it was a renowned local singer providing the entertainment and Miranda found herself caught up more than once in the beauty and emotion of the music. Enough to let down her guard and admit to Zamir at the end of the performance how much she enjoyed music.

'It must have been a big part of your life, since your mother was a professional singer.'

She nodded. 'There was always music in our house. Even before she returned to it professionally, my mother often sang.'

'And you sing too?'

'You'd think so, wouldn't you? But I can't hold a tune.'

She was surprised to see him frown. 'I heard an expert say everyone can sing in the right conditions.'

She sat back and folded her arms. 'Can you?'

He shrugged and without the least embarrassment launched into the beginning of a well-known ballad. His voice was deep and pleasant and sent a wave of tingling heat across her flesh as he held her eyes.

Miranda's breath stalled but she told herself she wasn't drawn to that dark gaze. Yet she'd swear there was softness in those velvety depths as he sang of yearning and thwarted desire.

'Bravo.' She applauded when he stopped after a few bars. 'You're a man of many parts.'

'Aren't we all? None of us are completely as we seem on first acquaintance.'

Miranda was surprised by that. As if he were a man slow to judge and willing to learn about people. Not an authoritarian ogre.

He leaned forward. 'Have you thought of having lessons since you enjoy music so much? I could arrange—'

'No! Thank you.'

He really *was* trying to build bridges. Miranda didn't know whether to welcome that or resist. But she was stuck here, at least until she found a way out of this preposterous situation. No matter where she ran she'd still be Zamir's wife. Even if she managed to get away from Qu'sil she'd be legally bound to him. He was right. She had to find a way to live with this.

Which meant accepting Zamir's olive branch.

'It wouldn't work. My mother tried to teach me.' Miranda winced at the painful memories. Her mother impatient and frustrated and she blinking back tears because she'd disappointed her mother. Now it was too late to win her approval. 'I'm told my singing sounds like a camel bellowing so I don't try any more.'

Zamir held her gaze and it felt, strangely, as if he saw something more than her sitting at the dining table. As if he saw her younger self, hurting. After a moment he changed the subject and she gratefully followed.

The next day he sent an invitation to afternoon tea. It was actually an invitation she wanted to accept.

'I'm meeting the Qu'sil Ladies' Equestrian Club,' she protested to her assistant. 'Surely I don't need to dress so ornately?'

The invitation said it was a small, private function. She'd been surprised and touched that Zamir should arrange this for her. He knew she was climbing the walls, being incarcerated.

Her assistant was adamant as she fussed over Miranda's stole. 'This is your very first engagement. You need to look both regal and bridal.'

Miranda surveyed her reflection doubtfully. She looked totally unlike herself in a long dress of deep rose pink with acres of gold embroidery on the sleeves and from the hem all the way up to her knees. A matching stole draped her head and shoulders. Around her neck was a heavy gold heirloom piece with a dozen crimson gemstones she feared might be rubies. She wore gold embroidered slippers and at least a dozen beautifully wrought gold bangles jingled on each arm.

Discomfort weighed heavily. And doubt.

All the horsewomen she knew were down-to-earth people. Some might look formally elegant in their dressage costumes but away from the public arena comfort rather than high fashion ruled.

This wasn't high fashion. This was blinding grandeur.

She shook her head, feeling the heavy gold earrings slap her neck. 'I still think I need to tone it down a bit. At least with the jewellery.'

'You don't want to let the Sheikh down, do you?'

Miranda bit her lip. She hated the situation Zamir had forced her into but embarrassing him in public wouldn't make that situation easier. Besides, over the last few days he'd tried to make her feel less over-whelmed. He'd even acquired a horse for her. A gorgeous Arab with excellent manners but enough spirit and energy to present some challenge.

The fact he'd organised for her to meet other horse-women showed goodwill and thoughtfulness, and a level of trust she hadn't expected. She couldn't repay that by deliberately flouting protocol.

Even her assistant, with her intricately done hair and heavy make-up, was more formally dressed than Miranda was used to. It must be a palace thing.

'Very well.' She loosened the stole and made for the door. She felt more than ever like an imposter but if that was what it took to spend time with other women who shared her interests...

She knew as soon as she joined Zamir in his office that something was wrong. His eyes widened before he looked away to close his computer. When he stood his expression was unreadable.

'Is everything all right?'

Miranda smoothed the folds of her heavy dress then stopped at the jingle of golden bangles. She didn't look like herself and she felt uncomfortable.

He inclined his head. 'Of course. You're ready?' He led her from his office towards the public reception rooms. 'I thought this would be a good way to ease into meeting people. Despite the name, it's not a formal society, but my sister's a member and I thought you'd have a lot in common.'

They approached a room that she knew to be a rela-tively small salon, merely big enough for fifty. A number of staff entered, carrying trays of food, and she caught the sound of female voices before the door closed.

Miranda stopped, impulsively reaching for Zamir. She only touched the sleeve of his dark suit then hastily let go as her skin tingled.

'You're anxious? There's no need. They all share your passion for horses.'

Miranda nodded. There *were* butterflies in her stomach. She'd never lost the expectation of being an outsider thanks to a lifetime of not quite fitting in anywhere but the stables.

But she never gave in to such nerves. She refused to cower in a corner.

'It's not that,' she murmured, then cleared her throat as she met his eye. 'Thank you, Zamir. Arranging this for me was thoughtful. I appreciate it.'

She couldn't remember the last time anyone had gone out of their way for her like this. It was usually her fitting in with others. This felt significant.

'It's my pleasure. I want you to be happy here.'

His mouth curled in that hint of a shadow of a smile and Miranda felt it as a rush of blood to the head. Would her bones melt if he smiled properly? It felt like it.

She shook her head. At her crazy imagination and at the idea of being happy here. As his wife. Preposterous!

But instead of growing angry, Zamir shrugged and led her forward. 'Shall we?'

Staff opened the door and they entered. There was silence for a moment, broken by a few gasps, then the shuffle of twenty women curtsying.

Women who tried, with varying degrees of success, to hide their surprise at the sight of her. Women in modern clothes, some in trousers and jackets, a couple in summery dresses, all looking stylish but undeniably comfortable.

Whereas she was trussed up like the tinsel-decked Christmas tree Matias always erected in December, the gaudier the better.

Heat rose to her throat and scorched her cheeks.

All her life she'd got the dress-up thing wrong. Her mother had looked effortlessly superb at all times and had eventually given up trying to mould Miranda in her image. Sadia could wear anything from traditional dresses to modern fashion and look totally at home. But Miranda could never pull it off. It didn't matter when she was in the stables, but in a royal court? In the public eye?

She felt gauche, an imposter in this place. Not the bride Zamir had wanted and, no matter what he said, she knew in her heart of hearts that no amount of coaching would make her fit.

No wonder Zamir had been surprised when he saw her. If only he'd told her how ridiculous she looked.

And what? You'd have raced back to change? It would have taken ages and you'd have been disastrously late.

He greeted the women, thanked them for coming. Then he introduced her and she stood straighter, pushing back her shoulders and fixing a smile that felt horribly false onto stiff lips.

She'd walked into her worst nightmare.

CHAPTER EIGHT

'I'M SORRY, MA'AM, but I can't open the gate.'

Miranda stared down at the uniformed guard whose expression was professionally blank. Beneath her Chico snorted and shifted his weight, lashing his tail as if he, like she, was desperate for a good gallop.

'I won't go far. I know there's a track that leads to a private section of coastline.'

She looked past the guard towards the deep blue of the sea and imagined herself racing along the shore. Exercise and, yes, speed, had long been her way of burning up an abundance of excess energy. Nothing soothed the nerves or overcame impatience like the wind on her face and the thunder of hooves, her heart singing at the sheer joy of uncomplicated physical exertion.

Instead she was cloistered in this palatial prison. It might have every luxury but it was still a prison.

'My apologies, but I have my orders. Under no circumstances—'

'It's all right.' She bit back a sigh. 'I understand.'

It would take more than a request from her to overturn an order from the Sheikh. Yet she stared at the controls for the vast wrought-iron gates. If she had a distraction...

The guard shifted, marching to stand with his back to the controls. Was she that obvious?

Probably. But she felt so hemmed in. Her skin itched with the need for freedom, if only temporary.

Reluctantly she turned away, urging Chico towards the wildest part of the vast grounds. There was space within the palace compound to gallop. It even had its own racecourse. But Miranda needed more, she needed to be away from this place, especially after this afternoon's events.

Her flesh crawled at the memory of her cringeworthy entrance to the afternoon tea earlier. Fortunately Zamir had been right and she'd ended up enjoying herself enormously.

After their initial wariness she and the others had relaxed and she'd been delighted to find herself with so many like-minded women. There was an equestrian trainer, an international dressage competitor, and a whole lot of others who took their riding seriously. Some had even started a programme similar to the one she'd been involved with in Argentina, providing riding opportunities for people with disabilities.

By the end of the session she'd been optimistic, feeling that with time she might find friends in the group.

Yet, as the door had closed behind them and she'd returned to her apartments to fling off her heavy, ornate clothes, she'd felt again that horrible sense of not belonging. What a gaffe, dressing for an intimate event as if she wanted to outshine everyone. Her assistant meant well but Miranda should have overruled her.

Except Miranda didn't trust her instincts when it came to clothes. She hadn't inherited her mother's innate stylishness and never managed to choose the right outfit for the social events to which her mother or her uncle had dragged her. Today reinforced her woeful lack of style. Even with a wardrobe full of designer clothes and a personal assistant she'd still got it wrong!

Her enforced seclusion hit harder than ever. Her guests had left but she alone wasn't allowed beyond the palace doors.

The mere thought of being cooped up made her want to scream and scratch and kick.

She hadn't done that since she was a child, after her father died and her mother left to live overseas. The adults had decided Miranda was better off in Aboussir in a settled environment. She was brought up by her father's family rather than following her mother's singing engagements from one city to another.

Never mind the fact her uncle had treated her like a changeling. An unwanted, untrustworthy foreign child who wasn't one of them.

Setting her jaw, Miranda touched her heels to Chico's flanks as they reached open ground. He leapt forward eagerly as if he shared her impatience.

It was late when they returned to the stables. She knew she'd missed a riveting tutorial on constitutional law. She'd have to apologise to the tutor. But even if she'd attended she'd have taken in little, too on edge to concentrate.

Miranda greeted the head groom, who'd finally been persuaded not to insist that one of the stable hands look after her horse. It was good to be able to do something for herself here. The familiar ritual of unsaddling Chico, rubbing him down, putting up the tack and checking his food and water was soothing.

She held out half a carrot, smiling as he whickered

his approval, his soft lips tickling her palm. 'You're a good boy, aren't you, Chico?'

'I thought his name was Zephyr?'

Miranda twisted around at the sound of that familiar, deep voice. She couldn't escape it, even in her restless dreams. Did he have to follow her here too?

Zamir was letting himself into the loose box, closing the door behind him.

The space shrank. That lovely feeling of muscle tiredness and calm that she'd worked hard to achieve disappeared in an instant. Every nerve was on alert, her pulse quickening as it did whenever he was near.

She looked away to Chico, crunching on his treat, almost wishing he were temperamental enough to shy and rear at a stranger in his box.

Some ally he was.

'That's his name, officially. But he reminds me of another horse I used to know.'

'Called Chico.'

She nodded, not bothering to explain that he'd been Matias's favourite. A veteran mount who'd died last year at a venerable age. Miranda had cried then, for it had felt as if she'd lost a family member. Zephyr's colouring was similar and so was the knowing gleam in his eyes. Miranda had looked at him and felt a rush of homesickness for all she'd left behind in South America. Not just the stables and her stepfather. His casual affection and steadfast trust meant so much. But also the sense of belonging.

'He answers to Chico.' She reached out and scratched the horse's hairy cheek. 'Don't you, boy?'

Chico lifted his head and stamped one hoof. She smiled. But the smile died when Zamir spoke again.

'You missed an appointment.'

'Not an appointment that *I* made.'

He said nothing and she swung around to discover he stood closer than before. Close enough that she had to tilt her chin to meet his eyes. That annoyed her, as if it were a physical reminder of the power imbalance between them.

'We went through that. These lessons are vital. You need to act as a queen. They're for your benefit, so you understand what's happening and can participate.'

'I don't want to participate.'

Miranda knew it was petty. She was in this situation and couldn't get out of it. Even Zamir couldn't get her out of it. But it was easier to argue than confront her new reality.

'You should have thought of that when you kidnapped me.'

Her body stiffened as if at the crack of a whip. That was the worst of it. If she hadn't interfered…

He was right. She had to wear the consequences of what she'd done. But *such* consequences!

It was impossible to be sanguine with her emotions all over the place. Especially when Zamir stood close, all the abrasive feelings she tried to conquer surged to the surface. He made her feel…not like herself. 'I'd rather not talk to you right now.'

'We have to talk some time, Miranda. I'm your husband.'

'In name only. I'm not really your wife. I'm…a chattel. A symbol, didn't you say? A convenience.'

He shook his head, his eyes narrowing. 'There's nothing in the least convenient about you.'

'Good.' She moved closer, thrusting her face into his

space, ignoring the rich spice and cedar aroma invading her nostrils. 'I'd hate to make things easy for you.'

She knew she wasn't being fair. She'd brought this on herself. He'd gone out of his way to make things easier for her. Introducing her to those women. Giving her Chico.

But those were just sops to his conscience because he'd trapped her in this appalling situation. He'd upended her life, giving her no choice, and expected her to go along meekly with his plans. Yes, she'd done wrong to kidnap him, but he'd done wrong, forcing her into this fiasco. They were both to blame. Yet it felt as though she was the one paying the heaviest price and she wasn't in the mood to be reasonable.

Zamir's nostrils flared, his eyes narrowing to glittering black slits.

The mere sight of him was a warning to back down. But if she backed down, she'd find it harder to stand up for herself later.

Everything was stacked against her. Even her senses that were enthusiastically cataloguing the sight, sound and scent of this man, as if in welcome, not rejection.

Miranda's head snapped back in horror.

'When will you finally accept that I'm not your enemy, Miranda?'

He lingered on her name, turning the vowels into music that produced a galaxy of goosebumps across her skin and a coil of desire low in her body.

She felt undermined. Trapped in uncharted territory.

'When you set me free. When you stop acting like my own private gaoler.'

Something flickered in those dark eyes. An emotion she couldn't read. His mouth twisted and the sharp planes of his face set like a rigid mask.

He looked daunting, imperious and frighteningly sexy.

'You know I can't set you free. It's impossible.'

He paused, chest swelling on a deep breath. When her glare didn't soften he shook his head.

'If you insist on treating me as the enemy...' His voice grated across her skin, drawing her nipples tight. As if that softly determined tone were instead an invitation to sensual pleasure beyond her imaginings. 'Maybe I should live up to your expectations.'

His hands closed around her upper arms and before she had time to process that, he pulled her to him. Her breasts pressed against his hard torso, her legs were between his, the heat of his groin searing her belly.

Lightning arced through her body, soldering her boots to the ground and turning her mouth arid.

Miranda swallowed and watched Zamir's eyes follow the jerky movement, then lift to her mouth when she slicked her lips.

His stare was needle-sharp. It should hurt her, or at the very least repulse her.

Instead it made her want.

She swayed, her palms flattening on his broad chest. To push him away, obviously.

But then she felt the heavy thump of his heart. Steady and even but quick, almost as quick as hers. Instead of pushing, her fingers curled into his shirt, her short nails raking.

She felt him jump, an infinitesimal twitch of muscles, enough to betray his response to her touch.

That was when it hit her that this was truly dangerous. Not because Zamir had the physical strength to force her into something she didn't want. Despite the disparity in their sizes and the raw masculinity that saturated the laden air between them, Miranda couldn't believe he'd use force.

The real danger was because she *did* want.

So much that it had grown into need. A need for more from this man. A need for something to quell the jittery sensation in her chest and stop the dragging heat inside as if her vital organs were melting on a tide of...

Lust.

The word hit at the precise moment his mouth covered hers.

Her head rocked back. Not with the force of his movement, but in instinctive denial.

She'd weathered kisses before, most unwanted, a few eagerly sought but soon disappointing. This was different. Miranda knew, with the desperate awareness of a hunted animal, that Zamir's kiss threatened her survival.

Yet her rejection was short-lived. So short she wondered if she'd imagined it, a salve to her pride.

Because now the feel of his lips on hers was...

She didn't have a word for it, just felt rising excitement deep inside.

He didn't force her mouth open, demanding submission. He merely slid his lips across hers. Once, twice, three times and that sensual slide threatened to blow the back off her skull.

She gasped, drawing in the taste-scent of hot masculinity and exotic spice.

Even then he didn't press home his advantage, plundering her mouth like a conqueror. To her bemusement he waited. So did she, expecting him to use, if not force, then heavy-handed persuasion.

Instead she felt only the caress of his breath and the surprising softness of his lips on hers. The drumbeat of his heart beneath her palm and the way the muscles in his powerful body stiffened. As if he held himself back.

Whatever game he played, he was better at it than she, but then recklessness had always been her besetting sin.

Unable to prevent herself, Miranda slid her mouth along his, tasting his bottom lip with the tip of her tongue.

Who knew a man could taste so delicious?

That was all it took. This was no longer a challenge or a battle of wills. It was…irresistible. Necessary.

When his tongue touched hers it was as if she'd waited for ever. Her mouth opened like a flower to the sun and what happened next took no thought at all. Their kiss was slow, an unhurried act of discovery. Yet there was no clumsiness, no bumping of noses. None of the self-consciousness she'd experienced when other men had kissed her.

It felt as if she and Zamir had kissed before. As if she'd been born knowing how to kiss him.

Knowing how to elicit that faint groan of approval deep in his throat as their caresses deepened. Just as he unerringly knew how to make her melt with each deft touch.

It was wondrous, addictive, and Miranda pressed closer, almost sighing with relief when those powerful arms encircled her and held her close.

Her hands slid up his chest to the warmth of his neck, fingertips questing into crisp short hair at the back of his head. A quiver of arousal shot through her, just from the friction of his hair against the pads of her fingers.

Or maybe it was from their deepening kiss, mouths fused together as hunger rose.

Zamir cupped the back of her head with one large hand as need became more urgent and she leaned back across his embracing arm.

That made her fully conscious of his impressive strength, the easy way he took her weight. Once the awareness of his greater power would have annoyed her. She gloried in it, arching further, her breasts thrusting against that hard chest. Her thighs braced against his.

Now the kiss held a demanding edge. Something akin to what she'd expected when he'd pulled her to him. But she welcomed it, clutching him close as if she could meld their bodies. Because this wasn't bullying domination. This was shared.

It was utter heaven.

Heat was a volcanic rush from her womb to her breasts, climbing her throat and dampening her hairline.

'Miranda.'

If she hadn't felt the vibration of his voice where her chest pressed to his, she might not have recognised it. It didn't sound like him. It was hoarse, stretched raw, and she loved it.

'Zamir,' she whispered against his lips. 'I—'

Something hit her, knocking her hip and shocking her eyes open to meet Zamir's blazing black gaze. For a second Miranda was lost in those midnight depths. She felt herself spinning out of control, until another knock and a strange sensation against her thigh.

Dragging her gaze from Zamir, she saw Chico's

twitching grey ears as he mouthed the pocket of her jeans, pretending to eat it.

The world tilted as Zamir straightened with her in his embrace. For a second longer their bodies were fused from chest to knee. Then he released her, lowering his arms slowly as if to be sure she wouldn't stagger.

Instantly Miranda stepped back, standing tall and gulping in breaths that didn't fill her lungs. Even though, seconds ago when her mouth had been plastered to his, she'd noticed no difficulty breathing.

That's because you didn't care then what he thought. You were too busy being swept away in the moment.

Now reality came crashing back.

'What was that?' she snapped, needing to fill the silence before Zamir did. 'You proving your superior skills as a seducer?'

Chico nuzzled her shirt and she rubbed his head, grateful for the endearingly mundane contact when her brain was spinning and everything she knew about herself turned topsy-turvy.

'Maybe I just kissed you out of curiosity,' she said when he remained silent. 'Did that occur to you? After all, they say know your enemy.'

Disapproval pinched his brow and he seemed to grow taller, towering over her.

It was true that she'd wanted to know what kissing him was like. Yet from the moment their mouths touched it had felt familiar in a way no previous kiss had. More than familiar. Right. Perfect. Her body still sang with the joy of it.

His eyes narrowed but that challenging stare was marred by his slightly reddened lips. Lips that looked that way because of *her*. Even the pulse pounding in the base of his neck was, she knew, at least partly the result of their shared ardour.

He might have initiated the kiss but *she'd* done that to him. They'd both been affected.

That felt like triumph and disaster.

Zamir rolled his shoulders. 'Are you saying you didn't enjoy it? Because if you are—' his stare turned piercing '—I'd have to call you a liar.'

Miranda stepped back, only to come up against the wall. Chico mouthed at her hip pocket, searching for carrots, but she couldn't pull her gaze from Zamir.

'You think you're such an expert you can read my mind?'

He shook his head. 'Not your mind, Miranda. Your body. It speaks the truth you're too scared to admit.'

His glorious mouth, which had led her to the edge of paradise, quirked up at one corner and she felt something—her ego perhaps—crash and splinter. For even that tiny change of expression made her want to return to those moments of bliss in his embrace.

'Your body says you want me. You wanted me a few minutes ago when you were in my arms. And you want me still. *That's* why you're lashing out. Because I made you face the truth.'

For the first time she could remember Miranda was bereft of words. When faced with a situation where she felt out of her depth her defence mechanisms had always been a quick riposte and a defiant act. Taking some risk. Proving her mettle. Showing she wasn't cowed.

This time words deserted her.

Once, long ago, she might even have thrown a punch, aiming to puncture his complacency. But Miranda knew with visceral certainty that if she touched him again, she might just prove the very weakness she wanted to deny.

Zamir shifted his weight, his arm lifting as if to reach for her, but she shrank back and he stiffened, his expression setting in cold, haughty lines.

In anger or disappointment?

'I'll leave you to finish up here.' He patted Chico on the neck and turned on his heel. 'We'll talk later, Miranda.'

When he was gone she wrapped her arms around Chico's neck and breathed in his comforting, horsey smell.

What was she going to do?

Zamir was right. She *did* want him. She who'd never wanted any man enough to take a lover.

She was in desperate lust with her autocratic, un-wanted husband.

CHAPTER NINE

'YOU SUMMONED ME?'

Zamir looked up from his computer to see Miranda in the office doorway. Heat gathered in his belly and his pulse quickened as he remembered her in his arms yesterday. Her sweet ardour had subverted his anger.

Miranda's insistence on always painting him in the worst possible light had grown wearing, finally puncturing his armour and making him want to forget the expectations placed upon him as a leader, a role model, a man who strove to do the best for others.

He'd wanted and he'd reached out to take, or at least to stifle her poisonous words. He'd tried to make things easier for her but that seemed to count for nothing.

Yet when he'd looked into her taunting, tense face, his annoyance had dimmed.

'Thank you for coming.' Zamir kept his voice even, ignoring his wayward thoughts and the provocative way she'd used the word *summoned*.

He'd let down his guard with her yesterday. He couldn't afford to do it again, at least not yet.

Would she wear that disapproving pout if she knew it emphasised the sultry invitation of her full lips?

As for her nonchalant stance, one hand on the door

she'd opened before knocking, one hip thrust forward in an attitude of feminine challenge...

It made him want to provoke her. He sensed it wouldn't take much to nudge her into reckless action. Confrontation seemed to rouse her fighting spirit. If he exasperated her enough maybe *she'd* initiate their next kiss.

Despite yesterday's scathing words and her disdain now, she couldn't hide the glitter of awareness in her fine eyes, or the way they lingered on his mouth. The air was alive and sparking and Zamir was experienced enough to recognise the charge of mutual attraction.

He punched down a surge of anticipation and stood.

She was a puzzle he needed to understand. Despite her antipathy, she hadn't tried to cause trouble publicly. When he'd rung her stepfather to introduce himself and allay concerns it was to discover she'd already called him. Whatever she'd said, the Argentinian seemed content.

Why had she smoothed things over? Because she'd finally accepted their marriage? Or because she didn't want to worry a man who couldn't change the situation?

'Please, come in and shut the door.'

For a moment she looked as if she might retreat.

That reminded Zamir of yesterday's suspicion that she was a relatively inexperienced kisser. The idea had kept him awake long into the night.

Finally Miranda turned and shut the door with exaggerated care. Did her choice of trousers and a khaki shirt signal she'd made no special effort for him? But the tailored trousers emphasised her toned form and the fine shirt clung to her breasts as she twisted. He recalled in devastating detail how those breasts had felt, pressed against him.

He cleared his throat and yanked his thoughts back to business. 'Please, take a seat.' He waited till she took an armchair before sitting opposite her. 'I need to ask you more questions.'

'Questions? About what?'

'About you.' Zamir smiled reassuringly, but instead of relaxing she sat straighter, fingers digging into the arms of her chair.

'What sort of things?'

Everything. He'd never met anyone so intriguing. He needed to understand her better so she wouldn't be able to take him by surprise or provoke him again. Zamir *had* to be in control, not acting impetuously.

'You've aroused a lot of interest. We need material to release publicly as required.'

'Who is *we*?'

'My team. We have specialists who deal with press releases, public engagements, the media and so forth.' He paused. 'Actually we should have done this as soon as you arrived.'

But for once he hadn't been totally pragmatic. He'd given her time to adjust. He suspected his uncle wouldn't have done so, but despite Afifa's fears, or maybe because of them, Zamir chose a more subtle approach. He'd hoped to win Miranda over with kindness and patience. So far he'd failed.

'You'll tell your staff anything I tell you?'

'Only what they need to know to do their job.' He watched her frown. 'They are there to help us. To manage your public image and pre-empt difficulties.'

'Difficulties?'

'There's enormous speculation about you. You aren't the woman I'd planned to marry.'

She opened her mouth then closed it again, as if remembering she was the reason he hadn't been able to marry Sadia. '*Enormous* speculation?'

He nodded. 'So the team needs to know more.' And because, while Zamir didn't have political enemies as such, there were powerful politicians who weren't above making trouble for the new Sheikh if it meant improving their positions. Disrupting the amalgamation of Aboussir and Qu'sil would be the perfect time. Already they'd tried to pressure him over some major development schemes and they'd love to find a chink in his armour. He couldn't afford for Miranda to be that chink. It was imperative her image, appearances and behaviour were appropriate.

'You're afraid I have scandalous secrets?'

'Do you?' Unlike her cousin, Miranda hadn't always lived under close supervision. Sadia's unblemished character had been part of her attraction as a royal wife.

Miranda held his gaze and he'd swear the air sizzled. He leaned closer, pulled by that same force that had drawn him to her yesterday. He felt the tingle of blood in his fingers, the heaviness in his belly—

'If I had secret scandals, I wouldn't share them with your media gurus.'

She turned towards the window.

Stonewalling wouldn't help. Not if there really was something important. He pulled out the typed pages and proffered them, making her turn back.

'What's this?'

'Your homework. We need answers to these questions. The media team has been bombarded with queries. Your answers will give them something to work with.'

She didn't respond, too busy scanning the pages.

'You need to know about my friends?'

'Once I'm crowned ruler you'll be my queen. With that comes responsibilities. For instance, if in future one of your friends wants to do business here, we want to avoid accusations of favouritism.'

Her eyes blazed more silvery than grey, just as they had in the stables yesterday. Grimly Zamir registered a spark of response deep in his belly. After yesterday's kiss his desire for her was impossible to ignore.

Confident women had always appealed to Zamir. He liked someone who could hold her own in conversation and in bed. Maybe it was a blessing in disguise that the match with Sadia hadn't gone ahead.

Except your wife hates you.

Yet maybe she protests too much.

Miranda had been ardent and enticing in his arms. Walking away from her yesterday had taken all his self-control. If it hadn't been for her horse interrupting, Zamir might have had her up against the wall.

He'd spent a restless night imagining just that.

Would she still be so argumentative if he had? Or would she be enticing him into bed?

'None of my friends would do that.' She interrupted his thoughts. 'Besides, they're not powerful.'

'What about your stepfather and his friends? Wealthy acquaintances you've met through horse training?'

She crumpled the papers. 'You can't expect me to list everyone I've ever worked with!'

'Do the best you can.'

'What, so they can be investigated?'

Zamir held back from saying that at least a cursory investigation of her past was inevitable. No point provoking more outrage. 'Not necessarily.' He rubbed a hand around the back of his neck. Why had he imagined, even for a moment, that she'd make this simple?

'Did you have to fill in a questionnaire too?'

He shook his head. 'There's no need. My life's an open book. I've lived at the palace since I was ten. I've been in the public eye since I was thirteen.'

'You must have secrets.'

He spread his hands. 'Who doesn't?'

'Tell me one.' She lifted her chin. 'Tell me a secret and I'll fill in your form.'

He frowned. 'A secret?'

She nodded. 'Not a state secret. I'm not interested in those. Something personal. Something no one else knows.'

It was crazy. His secrets had nothing to do with this.

But if it meant getting Miranda to co-operate, and, more importantly, winning her trust...

'A secret of mine and in return you answer the questionnaire and a question of mine,' he responded. 'But I won't share that answer with anyone.'

Her eyes widened, then he read a gleam of something there that might have been anticipation. 'No fair. If you want all that, I get to ask another question too.'

Why not? Letting her win this negotiation might help. She must have felt powerless these last few days.

Plus playing Q and A might tear down some of the barriers between them. After yesterday he was even more impatient to overcome her animosity. For the good of the country, of course.

And because he wanted her in his bed. Maybe after that he'd be able to devote his full attention to business.

'All right.'

'You agree?'

Zamir nodded, enjoying her almost comical look of disbelief. 'Fire away.'

She was silent for several moments. 'Why do you want to be Sheikh so much? I understand about the amalgamation of our countries. I don't mean that. I want to understand what it is about being supreme ruler that really appeals to you. What you get out of it.'

Zamir felt the air heavy in his lungs as her words sank in. His flesh prickled at the insinuation he was motivated by personal greed. For wealth, or power. Prestige perhaps. Sourness filled his mouth.

Strange how this proof that she saw him as a power-hungry politician hurt. She'd said as much before but Zamir had hoped she'd begun to understand.

'Aren't you going to answer?'

His vision cleared and he saw her, canting towards him, hands clasped and eyes serious.

The question wasn't malicious. She genuinely didn't understand him.

Whose fault was that?

'I've never *wanted* to be Sheikh. When I was younger I had other dreams. But I grew up. I was made to see the world as it is, not as I wanted it to be.'

Miranda's brow furrowed. 'I don't understand. Sadia said you moved to live with your uncle so he could teach you to be Sheikh. I thought—'

'That I made that choice?' He shook his head. She really had no idea. 'The choice was made for me before

I was old enough to have a say in it. When I was ten my parents died and my uncle brought us to live with him.'

In answer to her unspoken question he added, 'Us being my seven-year-old brother Umar and five-year-old sister Afifa. They're overseas but you'll meet at the coronation.'

'That must have been…hard.'

He inclined his head. 'Your father died when you were young too.'

'He did.' She swallowed, her expression softening.

She'd loved him, he realised.

He thought about his parents. Had he loved them?

He supposed so, but he'd never felt close to either. He and his siblings had been brought up by staff, though when they were orphaned, he'd done his best to be a surrogate parent for the others.

He'd learned more about love and nurturing from that than from his parents. Hours consoling Afifa or distracting her with childish games. Nights with one or both his siblings in his bed because they'd had bad dreams. Reading bedtime stories, mopping up tears and encouraging them when they didn't live up to their uncle's exacting standards.

'By the time I was twelve I was well on the way to being moulded by my uncle and tutors to take the throne. I found out later that when my parents died he'd been negotiating to marry again, in hopes of fathering an heir. But he gave that up when he adopted me, with Umar as a spare heir if needed.'

'So this was against your will?'

Zamir shook his head. 'It wasn't that simple. If my parents hadn't died, if my uncle had had a son of his own, then I'd have been happy as a private citizen. But fate set this road for me. There's no point dwelling on what would have happened if my life had been different.'

'Even if you don't want this?'

'It's not a matter of want. This is my duty, my role in life. I've trained hard for it. I'm good at it. Millions of people trust and rely on me. I can make a real difference in their lives. How many people can say that?'

Miranda scrutinised him carefully. 'And that's enough?'

Zamir couldn't hold back a grunt of laughter. Had she gone from believing him to be grasping, to feeling sorry for him?

'There are definite compensations. And yes, there's enormous satisfaction in being able to do good for my country.'

'It never occurred to you to step aside and pursue another dream? Let your brother take over?'

Zamir's amusement died. 'It's not an option.'

Miranda tilted her head like an inquisitive bird, eyes bright, expression intrigued. There was something about having her full attention, not her anger or indignation, but her curiosity and—was he kidding himself?—maybe her sympathy, that appealed.

He should tell her she'd already had more information from him than they'd bargained for. But he'd agreed to a second question. Umar wouldn't mind. Besides, Zamir needed to break down the barriers between them. If she understood his motives it could only help.

'My brother isn't cut out for the role.'

'Aren't you assuming a lot? If he had the chance—'

'He'd hate it. Umar is very bright. He's quick-witted, loyal and decent, but he has a short attention span for anything that doesn't interest him. School was a night-mare except for the subjects he loved. He'd rather be out, making things happen in his own way. The idea of him sitting through long debates or consultations on subjects he's not passionate about, much less putting up with royal protocol...'

Zamir shook his head. 'He couldn't wait to get away from palace life. He's thriving and making his mark in the world, drawing attention to injustice. The thought of him forced to give that up... No, I couldn't do that to him. He suffered enough, trying to live up to royal expectations when he was here.'

'I see.'

Just that. Did she see? Or did she believe, even now, that he twisted the truth to his own ends?

Miranda was reeling but struggled not to show it.

It had been convenient to paint Zamir as a selfish dictator, driven to grab power for his own ends.

But she'd seen his expression soften when he'd spoken of his family. When he'd described his brother, there'd been no mistaking his affection.

Zamir had been raised believing it his responsibility to look after his country, no matter what he personally wanted. That didn't absolve him from forcing her to marry, but it cast a new light on his motives. He wasn't as selfish as she'd imagined. His vehemence in protecting his brother's freedom was real.

In other circumstances she'd admire him. The re-alisation sucked the air from her lungs. It was difficult enough, fighting this intense physical attraction.

She had an awful suspicion her new understanding of his character would make that resistance tougher.

Miranda shot to her feet, clutching his questionnaire. 'If you want this answered today I'd better make a start.'

'Aren't you forgetting something? You were going to answer a question from me.'

Dark eyes searched hers and there it was again, the feeling he could see deep into her insecurities. Reluctantly she sank into her chair. A deal was a deal. She'd honour their agreement.

Miranda leaned back, crossing one leg over the other. 'Ask away.'

For the longest time Zamir studied her, then spread his hands. 'I'm torn. I should ask if it's likely someone will come forward with a kiss-and-tell story about you that we need to prepare for.'

Miranda stiffened. He wanted to know about her lovers. She had nothing to be ashamed of, making the choices that had been right for her. Yet she shied from revealing her virginity to this charismatic, obviously experienced man who evoked such unprecedented desires.

Not because she was bashful but because it was yet one more area in which he had the advantage over her.

His kiss had undone her and afterwards she'd resorted to anger rather than reveal that vulnerability. He'd sauntered away from that devastating encounter as if unaffected.

He hadn't spent the night unable to sleep for thoughts of what would have happened if Chico hadn't interrupted. *Wishing* Chico hadn't interrupted.

'But I also want to know why you gave up your studies. I know you were planning to become a teacher. But now you train horses instead. Did something happen... something that stopped you finishing?'

His expression was grave and the gleam in his eyes looked like sympathy.

He thinks there was some crisis. That something bad happened that prevented you continuing.

He was concerned on her behalf?

That couldn't be. Yet that really did look like compassion. Did he think she'd had some terrible trauma?

'Is this your way of trying to winkle out answers to two questions?'

His mouth curled in a rare smile that held no cynicism. Its impact was like an earth tremor rippling up from the polished floor, through her soles and shattering another level of her hard-won protective walls.

'Ah, caught in the act. I could point out that you asked me more than one question. But I'll just leave it to you to decide which you'll answer.'

When Zamir smiled he was a different man. As if clouds that had blocked the sun blew away, leaving glittering golden light. Revealing a face so appealing it almost hurt to look at him.

It was on the tip of her tongue to blurt out that he should smile more often and everyone would jump to obey his slightest wish. But they did that anyway.

It was unfair that this man had so many advantages. Power, looks, even charm when he chose to use it, while she had nothing but her wits.

'How did you know I studied to be a teacher?'

'My staff have done *some* background checking.'

She let that pass. Of course they had. 'It's no big secret. I just wasn't cut out to be a teacher.'

'You discovered that when you started your training?'

It would be easy to agree and leave it at that but Miranda felt she owed him honesty. He'd been frank with her, letting her glimpse his private world. Besides, the way he described his brother made her wonder if he might understand better than her family had. She'd been a disappointment both to her uncle and her mother. Only Matias accepted her as she was, never pushing her to be someone different.

Are you really so needy that you want Zamir's approval?

But she owed him something. Despite everything, he'd been kind, arranging that afternoon tea and giving her privacy. He was trying. Pride demanded she accept that.

Miranda looked at the crumpled papers on her lap and smoothed them out. 'I knew before I enrolled. I didn't want to be a teacher. Not in a school anyway. I enjoy helping people learn to ride and care for animals but that's different.'

She looked up. 'I was never good at school, except for sport. Most lessons bored me and the thought of studying for years just to end up in a classroom again… It wasn't for me.'

She shook her head. 'When you spoke about your brother, I could relate to him.' She hurried on. 'I'm not claiming to be brilliant like him but I like to be hands-on. There are things I enjoy. Like being with animals, training and rehabilitating them after injuries. Helping kids, and adults for that matter, develop self-confidence through riding. But make me write essays? No, thanks.'

'So why enrol?'

'Family pressure.' Like him, she realised. 'My mother had hoped I'd take after her and be a glamorous singer or actress, but she had all the talent in the family.' Her mother had loved her in her own way but hadn't known what to do with a daughter so different to herself. Plus by the stage Miranda left school her mother had met Matias and had other priorities.

'I was living with my Aboussi family and my uncle said I either needed to marry or get qualifications to support myself. I chose the latter. Sadia enrolled in a teaching degree and it was one of the few careers my uncle approved of for us.'

Zamir's mouth flattened. 'He's very old-fashioned.'

Miranda nodded. 'He was almost apoplectic when I withdrew and moved overseas. Later, when he heard I was working in a professional stable, he all but disowned me.'

Gruff laughter scraped her body like the brush of suede on bare skin. 'Think how his nose must be out of joint now that you've married me and will soon be Queen.'

Her lips quivered. 'I hadn't thought of that.' She'd been too focused on her situation to spare a thought for him.

'See?' Zamir's smile did devastating things to her insides. 'There are compensations to our marriage.'

Her mouth kicked up at the corners in answering amusement.

'Speaking of our marriage, we'll make a public appearance in front of the palace the day after tomorrow. It's time I presented you to our people. But don't worry, you won't have to say anything. Just stand at my side and smile.' He paused. 'My staff will talk with yours about appropriate clothes.'

Because she couldn't be trusted to get that right.

Miranda shrank inside.

Despite what Zamir had said about there being no way out of their marriage she'd hoped for a loophole. But once she'd been shown off like some prize acquisition in a no doubt televised event, there'd be no escape.

She'd be Zamir's wife for real.

With difficulty she swallowed over a jagged obstruction in her throat.

The scary thing was that a tiny part of her was excited at the idea of him claiming her as his wife. Because he'd awoken such a longing for intimacy, for *his* touch, that she felt like a stranger in her own body, ready to ignore the negatives of her situation if he'd only ease her growing need.

Miranda shot to her feet. 'I'll go and start on these questions.'

He stood and something in his intent expression warned her he guessed at her weakness. She couldn't bear that.

She stepped out of reach then made herself pause and send him a sideways glance that she hoped looked insouciant.

'As for previous lovers with kiss-and-tell stories...' He stilled, apparently riveted by her words. She shrugged. 'I'm afraid I can't make any guarantees.'

Strictly it was true. She'd never had a lover. Yet she'd heard of people falsely claiming intimacy with public figures, seeking attention or money.

It was a petty thing to do, implying lies about her past. But she was tired of being on the back foot, the inexperienced, gauche one. The one who had to make up ground to be good enough.

With a tight smile she turned and strolled from the

room. It was only when the door closed behind her that her shoulders hunched and her mouth flattened at the prospect of what was to come.

CHAPTER TEN

'You look stunning.'

Zamir's words escaped unbidden, stopping Miranda inside the door of his salon.

Her bright eyes widened as they locked on his and a blast of heat shot through him, settling low in his belly. His pulse thundered and all thoughts of the speech he was about to make fled.

No sign now of the argumentative opponent so ready to take umbrage. His bride looked willowy, womanly and utterly desirable.

Her clothing drew attention to the spare, pure lines of her face, her grace and the lush promise of her mouth.

It took such effort to drag his gaze from her lips.

Her dress was silver, long and embroidered with tight sleeves that widened towards the wrist. Over her dark hair she'd draped a sheer scarf the same colour as the antique pearls that clustered in rows around her neck and wrists.

'You don't need to lie, Zamir. I don't need the pep talk. I'm fully prepared to go out there with you.'

Her tone made it sound as if he were about to lead her into a pit of desert vipers, instead of merely to a podium before the palace where the crowd could see them.

The numbers out there had surprised Zamir. He'd expected a huge crowd to witness the coronation, still weeks away. But it seemed everyone was agog with curiosity to see his bride.

Miranda swallowed and his attention dropped to her slender throat. She was a confusing mix of vulnerable and determined. Now he noted her tightly clasped hands and pushed-back shoulders. She was anxious and determined not to show it.

Did she really have no idea how she looked? Or how his people would joyfully welcome his bride?

'Have I ever lied to you, Miranda?' His voice was rasping, betraying his growing hunger. For this woman who challenged him, hated him even, but enticed him too.

Hell! He hoped she didn't still hate him.

Yesterday he'd even found himself jealous of her horse! Zamir had wanted her to stroke him and whisper sweet nothings in his ear with as much enthusiasm as she gave her equine friend.

'But I…' She shook her head as if still not convinced.

'Surely you've been complimented on your appearance before.' It was impossible all the men in Aboussir and Argentina were blind.

She drew herself up. 'No. At least, only by men trying to get into my pants.'

His splutter of laughter was unstoppable. The disdainful twist of her mouth said everything.

'You didn't like them?'

What about the ex-lovers she'd hinted might come out of the woodwork now she was famous?

Her expression of regal scorn would have done his uncle proud. 'I don't want to talk about them.'

Zamir was perplexed. Had she really not believed the compliments she'd received? Why? For every new piece of information he had about Miranda he found another puzzle.

'Then we won't talk about them. But believe me, you look marvellous. Every inch the royal bride.'

'Thank you,' she said after a long pause that made him wonder if he'd somehow said the wrong thing. 'You brush up well yourself.'

He wished he could be sure that was admiration in her quick glance. It felt like it.

Or are you so used to feminine interest you're seeing it when it's not there?

No. He couldn't be mistaken, not after that kiss. He'd tapped a deep vein of desire when Miranda had kissed him back. If they hadn't been interrupted...

But royal Sheikhs of Qu'sil didn't have quickies in the stables.

No matter how much they wanted to.

It would have been unbecoming in his new role. More, he owed his bride better than a roll in the hay.

At least the first time.

The memory of their passion, the idea of forgetting decorum and slaking his hunger right there in the stables, stirred his libido. Zamir dragged oxygen into his lungs, pushing away the insidiously tempting image of Miranda, up against the wall with her legs around his waist while he drove them hard to a peak of pleasure.

Deliberately he turned to his desk as if referring to a document there, needing time to collect his wits and force down his burgeoning erection.

His mouth curled mirthlessly. That was *not* how his people needed to see him. He had to remember his uncle's example, the expectations upon him, the responsibilities he shouldered. The gravitas of his position.

When he turned back to Miranda he was in control of himself, at least on the surface. He couldn't afford to betray the desperate lust scrabbling at his vitals like a clawing, caged animal.

When Zamir turned back his expression was aloof. For a second, when he'd called her stunning, Miranda's heart had leapt. Because in that moment she'd imagined he looked dazzled.

Wishful thinking.

She'd had a lifetime of people's surprise when they discovered she was her mother's daughter, but with none of her mother's luminous blonde beauty and charm.

A tomboy, her mother had called her, in a tone that was half laughing, half disappointment.

Of course Zamir hadn't been dazzled. Stunning probably referred to her clothes, not her.

Even if, when she'd looked in the mirror, Miranda had for the first time in her life felt beautiful.

Zamir's gaze skimmed her but didn't settle. Not like a man appreciating a lovely woman. He'd said what he knew she wanted to hear.

He was good with words but his eyes told a different story. She felt a pang, wishing she really were as splendid as her fine clothes.

You are. No matter what anyone thinks, you're special. You've made a rewarding and satisfying life.

Which she'd had to leave behind.

'Are you ready?'

She nodded.

'Excellent. The crowd will be excited to see us but

there's no reason to be alarmed. All you have to do is smile.'

Given her stiff facial muscles, Miranda wasn't sure that was possible.

It was as well she didn't have to speak. Her larynx closed and her breath came in quick gasps as she saw the enormous throng surrounding the palace. Her suite was on the far side of the building and she'd had no idea there were this many people in the capital.

The horrible feeling that she was an imposter hit again full force.

She didn't fit here. She hadn't even mastered the art of walking in high heels, much less being royal! Would they see through her? Or would her fabulous clothes be enough camouflage if she stood tall?

'They've been gathering for hours,' Zamir murmured as they walked from the palace into the vast forecourt beyond which the people waited. 'Some have travelled from the furthest provinces.'

A hush descended that made Miranda's nape prickle. It seemed impossible that such a huge gathering should be so silent. Then someone called out Zamir's name and the crowd erupted into cheers and ululations of celebration.

'They like you,' she whispered when she found her voice. This was no orchestrated show of support. This was real and overwhelming.

'They like what I stand for. Stability and good government. Like my uncle before me.'

But Miranda wondered. He said he'd been in the public eye since he was thirteen. He'd spent years deputising for the failing Sheikh. Hearing snippets of conversation among household staff, Miranda knew people admired Zamir because of who he was, not simply because of his title.

They reached a raised platform. Above it an awning of golden silk rippled in the light breeze. Miranda lifted her long skirt a little, needing to see where she stepped in her unfamiliar high heels.

That was when she almost came to grief, her narrow heel slipping sideways on the second step and her ankle turning abruptly. She reached out to grab for a railing that wasn't there but was saved by Zamir.

He gripped her upper arm, holding her steady. She looked up to see him leaning close, concern in his eyes.

Concern that you don't make a laughing stock of yourself and therefore him.

Yet the negative voice faded as Miranda met his eyes.

'Sorry. These stairs need treads and a hand rail. It will be arranged for next time.'

She exhaled slowly and nodded, hyper-conscious of his touch through her gown. 'I'll just concentrate on getting through this time.'

His smile was pure reassurance yet it felt intimate. And it dragged up all the longing she'd tried to suppress. A longing she shouldn't feel for this man.

They walked up the steps together, Zamir still holding her arm. To her astonishment, when they reached the platform, instead of removing his hand, he slid it down her sleeve and threaded his fingers through hers.

His hand was warm, dry and reassuring, which must be why he did it. He must have seen her tremble and known she was nervous.

Zamir led her to the microphone and addressed his people. What he said was a blur. Miranda concentrated on nodding and smiling in response to the cheers that erupted whenever he paused. And standing firm on her own two feet.

Trust her to have stumbled. Since her mother died she'd made almost a virtue of avoiding occasions where she had to dress up. She should have practised wearing high heels again instead of telling herself she wanted no part of today's event. She'd known she couldn't avoid it but had pretended it didn't matter.

But Miranda couldn't run from this any longer. Zamir and the people who expected so much from him were her reality now. She saw, heard and felt their enthusiasm and trust for him, their willingness to accept her because he'd chosen her.

Being here, basking in the reflected glow of all that positivity made her understand a little of his determination to be the man his people needed. Even made her want to help, or at least not hinder.

She had to face facts. Much as she abhorred their forced marriage, she didn't abhor Zamir or what he stood for. In fact he was proving the sort of strong, honourable yet understanding man her father had been.

Instead of being obstinate and reckless about things she couldn't change, she needed to adapt and learn.

'All done,' he murmured in her ear, the crowd going wild as he leaned close.

Miranda felt that powerful beat of attraction, her attention dropping to his perfectly sculpted mouth. The mouth that had been so gentle yet devastating on hers.

'Shall we go?'

She blinked and saw him survey her curiously, as if he couldn't understand why she was standing there staring with half the country's population and a massive TV audience watching.

'Sounds good. These clothes are getting heavy.' They weren't really. Miranda had found the dress and jewellery surprisingly comfortable and she loved the lustre of the pearls against her skin.

With one last smile for the crowd, she turned and they descended the steps. They were on their way back to the palace when bright colour caught her eye.

At the front of the crowd, not far away, a couple of young children held stems of bright yellow sunflowers, taller than themselves. They saw her notice and beaming smiles split their faces as they waved the flowers.

'Can we go over, Zamir? They must've waited ages and it's such a sweet gesture.'

He paused then squeezed her hand and turned towards them. The handholding was undoubtedly for the benefit of the public but she didn't mind. She rather liked it.

Wasn't that a scary thought?

Maybe that was why she moved faster, needing the distraction of the children. Others joined them now, wriggling between the adults. Children of all ages, one with a football under his arm.

The crowd jostled. There was a cry of alarm and the football shot out from the crowd.

Miranda just had time to see the horror on its owner's face when the ball was on her. She felt Zamir move as if to step in front of her but before he could she lifted the hem of her dress and stopped the ball with one sandalled foot.

A hush fell. She felt it like a weight across her shoulders and prickling on her skin. Thousands of eyes were on her, standing there with her dress of silver tissue hiked up around her shin, balanced on one high heel, Zamir's hand tight around hers.

Miranda didn't look his way, not wanting to see his disappointment that she'd wrecked her image of royal elegance. It was too late for that, so she did what she would have done if she were simply Miranda Fadel. She gently tapped the ball straight back to its owner.

For a second the crowd held silent then a great buzz rose. She couldn't hear what they said but she could imagine. The sort of disapproval her uncle had meted out so often, that she was too tomboyish, too wild, not quietly feminine enough.

'Come on,' Zamir urged. 'They're waiting for us.'

She stumbled forward, grateful for his grasp when seconds ago, concentrating on the ball, she'd had no difficulty balancing.

Fortunately the children didn't notice anything amiss. They were too keyed up with excitement to be judgemental. Gap-toothed grins abounded as eager hands pressed the sunflowers upon her. She heard Zamir greet the children and was grateful he carried the situation so easily. Despite the enthusiasm of the kids, she felt horribly self-conscious.

'My lady, my lady. Will you sign it, please?'

There, before her, was a dusty football.

'I don't—'

She turned to Zamir, seeking guidance and discovered him looking relaxed. He was probably regretting he'd been forced to marry her rather than her decorous and decorative cousin, who could be trusted to behave perfectly in public, but he hid it well.

'I don't have a pen on me. But...' He turned and

one of the security staff held out a pen, which Zamir passed to her.

'Thank you.'

Miranda scribbled her name and passed the ball back. She was kept busy accepting more flowers, until her arms were full and a staff member had to take some. But gradually she found her voice again, responding increasingly easily to the children. She spent a lot of time working with young people and their enthusiasm broke down barriers, even if she was aware of the adults standing back, surveying her. Critically? Most probably.

Finally Zamir took her hand again, thanking the crowd and saying goodbye.

He kept hold of her as they returned to the palace. Some image consultant had probably told him to. Which made her tug free as soon as the large doors closed behind them. It felt wrong that she enjoyed his touch so much when it was just a PR exercise.

From the corner of her eye she saw him frown but he merely led her back through the corridors to the private salon they'd used earlier.

The door had barely closed behind them when she said, 'It wasn't intentional, really. I didn't mean to disrupt everything.'

'Disrupt everything?'

His scrutiny made her blood rush faster, creating a heat far greater than she'd experienced outdoors.

'Stumbling on the stairs. Hoiking up my dress to play football, then being asked to sign it!' She swung around to face him. 'I'm sure you've never had to do that.'

Zamir met flashing silver eyes. They made him think of summer lightning turning the night sky brilliant. That was how he felt, as if a blast of energy exploded inside him. It threatened to scramble his thoughts.

He should be getting back to work. There was so much still to do. Yet all he could think of was Miranda.

'You're right. I've never had that honour.'

The only things he'd been asked to sign were boring legal documents. Never had he been asked to sign a souvenir like some sporting star.

Yet Miranda didn't look triumphant. When the corners of her mouth dragged down it wasn't in a pout or a tantalising smile, but a grimace. Her breasts rose high and quick as if she couldn't catch her breath.

'I'm sorry. Truly.' Her hands twisted and he realised, belatedly, that she was upset. 'You probably won't believe it, but I didn't deliberately try to sabotage today.'

He frowned. 'Sabotage?'

'By making a spectacle of myself.'

Zamir covered her restless hands with his.

That felt better. Outside he'd held her to steady her, but feeling her fine tremors he'd been hit by remorse.

She wasn't ready for this, hadn't had the benefit of years of training. She'd been thrust into an overwhelming situation with virtually no preparation. The lessons she had on court etiquette, local customs, history and laws weren't enough to prepare for a scene like today.

He rubbed his thumb across her wrist, feeling her racing pulse.

He wanted to ease her agitation. At the same time, just like earlier, he wanted physical contact. He'd been disappointed when she'd ripped her hand away as soon as they'd entered the palace.

'You didn't make a spectacle of yourself.' He peered

down into her flushed face. 'You do realise, you were a huge success?'

'Success?'

Had she heard the crowd? Seen the grinning adults as she'd interacted with the children? She acted as if she'd done something wrong.

Then he remembered her dismay when she'd worn that over-elaborate outfit to the afternoon tea he'd arranged. She'd looked aghast, which had surprised him. He'd believed nothing could faze Miranda. Even being blackmailed into marrying a stranger hadn't dimmed her spirit.

The only time he'd heard her sound less than sure of herself was when she'd spoken of her family. Of her mother's disappointment that Miranda didn't turn out to be a glamorous singer like her.

He frowned.

'Of course, a success. Everyone loved you. Not only did you appear like a fairy-tale princess, but you showed yourself to be something much more interesting. You connected with those children. You broke with royal protocol to mingle with them and then you topped it off by proving with that professional stop that, even in heels, you're a football natural. You do realise it's one of our national games, don't you? I suspect there will be a lot of children tonight asking if they can join a local club.'

Miranda scowled. He should be used to it, but this time there was no anger in her stare. He sensed merely confusion.

'I'm glad the costume did the trick.' She swallowed and looked over his shoulder. 'I felt...like an imposter wearing all this finery. But as for breaking with protocol.' Her eyes met his. 'I didn't realise I wasn't sup-posed to talk to the people. I read the briefing but I didn't see—'

'It probably wasn't in there because I was going to guide you. If anything *I'm* the one who broke with tra-dition by agreeing when you suggested talking with the children.'

'Why did you?'

Because she'd looked at him with those diamond-bright eyes, eager and excited, and he hadn't been able to resist.

'It seemed like a good idea at the time.'

Her mouth twitched. 'That's what I used to say when-ever I got in trouble for doing something wrong as a kid.'

'Did that happen often?'

'Often enough.' Her expression turned serious. 'So what I did really wasn't a problem?'

It surprised him that she still needed reassurance. He released her fingers and stroked his hands up her arms, stepping closer. 'It was a stroke of genius. Our country is a modern one but the rules around royalty haven't changed in a long time. It's time they did. You saw how the crowd reacted at the chance to be near you.'

'Near *us*.'

Zamir shrugged. He was popular with his people but it was she who'd been a hit today. 'You connected with them, Miranda. First you stunned them with your beauty then won them over by being down-to-earth, warm-hearted and real. All the parents watching you interact with their children knew you weren't faking.'

'I…' She shook her head. 'That's one of the nicest

things anyone's ever said. About being warm-hearted and down-to-earth, I mean.'

Her eyes met his and there was no attempt to hide her feelings. Zamir felt a rush of blood to his head, dazzled by what looked like joy and gratitude. And more, a glow of pride.

How often had Miranda received compliments? He'd guess not often enough.

'And you're beautiful,' he added deliberately.

Her eyes widened and he felt her retreat a little.

As if she didn't believe him?

Zamir had made his share of mistakes, including with Miranda. He'd come to realise that his bride was *far* more complex than he'd initially thought.

'I don't lie, Miranda. You're one of the most beautiful women I've met.'

She shook her head, that diaphanous stole slipping down to reveal close-cut curls that complemented her vibrant sexiness. She looked fresh and real and enticingly sensual. His fingers itched with the need to stroke those soft locks.

'It's just the fancy clothes. I'm not really—'

'You're not listening, Miranda.'

His fingers curled around her toned upper arms, registering through the fabric the vitality that was characteristic of the woman. As was her refusal to heed what he said.

She frustrated and aroused him in equal measure.

Maybe not equal. For now he drew in her scent—jasmine and warm woman—and arousal outstripped anything else. Except the need to make this absolutely clear.

'You're beautiful, Miranda. Whether you're wearing rich clothes or jeans and riding boots. It's not your clothes or how you wear your hair. Your beauty is in your bones and flashing eyes. In the way you carry yourself. Even in your temper.' He paused, knowing his admission gave her power but unable to deny it.

'It's the sort of beauty that will grow over the years. You'll still look elegant and sexy decades from now.'

'Sexy?'

Zamir's attention dropped to her mouth. Her lips were parted in surprise. Or invitation. An invitation his hardening body was eager to accept. A shudder ran the length of his backbone and down through his belly. A shudder of sexual arousal.

Abruptly he realised how close he held her. And the promise he'd given, that *she* would be the one to initiate intimacy.

'Definitely sexy,' he growled as he released her and stepped back, fingers flexing as if objecting to the fact they no longer held her. 'Too sexy. But I'm a man of my word.'

'You want me.'

He couldn't tell if it was a question or a statement, just knew he had to remove himself from her presence because this conversation eroded his control. 'We'll discuss it later.'

He turned towards the door then jolted to a stop. When her hand closed around his arm.

CHAPTER ELEVEN

MIRANDA LOOKED UP into his set features.

Haughty, she'd have called them a few days ago.
Grim. Forbidding.

Ridiculously appealing.

Now she realised something new. This stern look
wasn't from anger or disapproval. It was because he
struggled against the same desire she did.

He wanted her.

Admired her, even.

He hadn't been buttering her up with soft words to
make her more malleable. She'd read his frustration,
even indignation at her refusal to accept his compliments.

She'd heard honesty in his voice and read it in the
way he looked at her when he described her as beautiful.

That had stolen her breath.

All her life she'd been compared unfavourably with
her glamorous mother and beautiful, docile cousin. To
the extent that when men *had* complimented her she'd
written off their words as flummery, designed to win
her over because they wanted sex.

Zamir wanted sex—she'd read that white-hot flash

of hunger—but instead of capitalising on his compliment, he tried to walk away.

He was the most frustrating man!

She wanted to learn more. Experience more. She'd been on tenterhooks for days because, for the first time in her life, she had a genuine crush on a man. On her husband!

And now he wanted to end this fascinating conversation and leave her thwarted and unsatisfied.

From her youth she'd felt comfortable with boys, playing football or hanging around the stables, more at home there than inside her uncle's home, pretending to be a delicate flower. As an adult she'd worked with men, generally managing to downplay her gender by being as competent as them.

And because none of them made her heart race the way Zamir did.

It wasn't because he'd said she was beautiful. Though that had stunned her. For it had been more than a throwaway compliment. She'd seen honesty in his eyes when he'd talked of an intrinsic beauty rooted in character not clothes.

There was something about him that, from the first, had made her aware of him as male and herself as female, stirring up unfamiliar yearnings.

She cleared her throat. 'Don't go.'

He didn't move but nor did he relax. 'It's best that I do. It's getting late and—'

'Are you afraid to be alone with me?'

A muscle jumped under her touch and she watched his jaw flex, a pulse flickering at his temple.

'Afraid?' He shook his head. 'Hardly. I don't have anything to lose here.' He moved closer, right into her space so she had to raise her chin to hold eye contact. 'But you do. You're the one who doesn't want a sexual relationship.'

He was giving her the chance to withdraw.

To run away to her own rooms and pretend Zamir meant nothing to her.

But running away wasn't Miranda's style. No matter how unexpected or inconvenient, she wanted her husband.

'What if I've changed my mind?'

She felt him stiffen, saw his shoulders lift on a deeply indrawn breath. Those inky eyes narrowed. 'I'd ask if you were sure.'

Sure she was doing the right thing? She didn't feel sure of anything. Except that she could no longer ignore the craving that had become a compulsion.

Since she'd met Zamir every dormant feminine desire had grown supercharged. She wanted, *needed*, to share herself with him.

'I'm sure. I want you, Zamir.'

Her words fell into reverberating silence, unbroken so long that her breath hitched and her skin crawled. Had she misjudged him? Had he simply wanted to manoeuvre her into admitting—?

Her thoughts cut off as he leant down, his hands sure yet gentle as they cupped her cheeks, long fingers tunnelling through her hair. Ebony eyes locked on hers and she lost herself in their depths.

His lips brushed hers, once, twice, before settling, his tongue gliding across the seam of her mouth until she opened for him.

Everything changed. Need exploded as he delved deep and suddenly they were devouring each other, heads angling for better access, bodies pressing, hands grasping. She tasted his grunt of satisfaction as she wriggled between his spread thighs, registering the long column of his arousal jutting against her.

Heat saturated from her hairline to her toes, and especially in her womb where a hollow throb started up. She shifted her weight, circling her hips and Zamir groaned.

The sound was so raw that it fed her response. Her peaked nipples pressed against him and between her legs she felt a softening.

He skimmed a hand down her back, planting it against her buttocks and drawing her up against the tantalising hardness of his erection.

Miranda strained higher, dislodging his head scarf, clutching his thick, soft hair. It must be the only soft thing about him.

She moved against him and excitement edged with trepidation shot through her as she realised the size of his erection.

'I want to see you,' she whispered against his mouth.

She wanted to see all of him, experience everything.

He leaned back just enough to meet her eyes. 'I want to see you too. Let's go to my—'

'No!' She needed Zamir. Now. Here. Before she had time to second-guess the wisdom of sharing her body with the man who held all the power in this relationship. 'I want you *now*.'

His mouth kicked up in a smile that dragged sensation through her body like fingers through fur. She trembled.

'I love a woman who knows her mind.' His voice hit a baritone note that somehow heightened her tension.

Before she could protest he stepped back, leaving her body bereft. But he merely strode to the door, locking it.

'Take off your clothes, Miranda.'

She reached for the buttons at the back of her neckline as he toed off his shoes. Eyes holding hers, he hauled off his ceremonial robes, not pausing until he'd stripped bare, and she couldn't repress an awed gasp.

Zamir was tall and well built, broad across the shoulders, narrow at the hips, with strong thighs and a jutting erection.

She swallowed hard, her mouth dry at the symmetry and sheer magnificence of his virile body.

'Do you need help?' He walked towards her and her throat clogged. Instead of answering she nodded, unable to tear her gaze away.

Then he was before her. She was so close to all that bronzed skin, inhaling his distinctive scent, now mixed with something earthy that made her tremble with anticipation. Male pheromones.

'Let me.' Gentle hands on her shoulders turned her around then he swore under his breath. 'Who put in all these buttons? Haven't they heard of zips?'

His exasperation pierced her breathlessness and a laugh bubbled up. Then she felt him fumble with the tiny buttons as she had and her amusement died. Zamir seemed just as clumsy as she. Wishful thinking? Yet it reinforced the feeling that this was as significant for him as for her.

'It's no good. I haven't got the patience to undo them all.'

The fabric parted and callused hands slid across her upper back, making her shiver with voluptuous delight as the silk slid off her shoulders.

Warm lips pressed her nape then descended her spine, making her arch as sparks of arousal exploded at each point of contact. The bodice of her dress dropped just enough that he could slide her arms free of the sleeves. Then he was cupping her breasts in her bra, pulling her back against him. Miranda felt as if she'd died and gone to heaven.

'More,' she breathed.

'Demanding woman.'

But she heard his approval and when he snicked open her bra and tugged it free, taking her breasts in his big hands, his sigh of pleasure eclipsed hers. The sensation was so amazing, so exquisite, Miranda cupped his hands with hers, holding tight as if afraid he might let her go.

He caught her nipples between thumbs and index fingers, gently rolling them, and it felt as if she flew too close to the sun, cascades of sparks igniting and coalescing to burn bright and hot.

Miranda juddered, sinking back against him, luxuriating in the sensation of flesh against flesh. Even the soft scratch of his chest hair against her upper back undid her.

'More,' she gasped, twisting her hips and pushing back towards his groin.

'I'd imagined our first time being in bed.' His voice was so thick it took a moment to register what he said. 'But since you're so eager...'

Zamir removed his hands and the loss was so intense it stunned her. Before she could protest though, he lifted her and laid her down on a gilded sofa. The fabric was cool against her upper back and her long skirts still covered her legs. Except now, perched on the edge of the sofa, he slid his hands up her ankles, her shins, knees and thighs, lifting the silvery fabric to bunch around her hips.

'Beautiful,' he murmured. His attention was on the lace covering her mound, then flicked up to her breasts, bare and wobbling with each scant breath. Finally his gaze rested on her mouth and she felt it like a kiss.

A great shudder ran through her as their eyes met again. Falling into that glittering midnight gaze felt even more intimate than when he touched her with his hands or bare body.

Holding her gaze, he touched her again, fingers curling around her lace underwear, dragging it down her legs and off.

Miranda released a breath she hadn't realised she'd held.

Finally. She reached for him but he'd moved. Sliding down the sofa, he planted his palms on her bunched-up skirt and bent his head.

Hot breath tickled sensitive flesh, making her twitch and shift her legs apart. He smiled then, smug, but Miranda didn't mind. She just wanted more.

When he gave it to her, his mouth against her most sensitive flesh, she almost jolted up off the cushions. That slow, lingering touch unleashed something she knew instinctively had the power to devastate her. Something she feared might be addictive.

Before she had time to make sense of that he did it again, and again, and she was moving with him, body undulating. Her breath snagged in her lungs, her hands anchored in his dark hair.

The air changed, thickening and growing heavy as if at the approach of a storm. Was that the crackle of thunder or an auditory illusion caused by her rampaging pulse? Her heart swelled as if it might burst free from her chest. Finally relief came, searing, blinding white light and sensations of pleasure almost too intense to bear.

Over the thunder in her ears, Miranda heard a high keening sound as she shuddered in ecstasy.

Then finally, Zamir lay over her, his mouth against her, murmuring praise and reassurance, his weight anchoring her to the world again, bringing her back to herself.

Miranda wrapped her arms around his ribcage, holding him close as he stroked the hair from her face and kissed her ear, cheek and neck. She shivered as those caresses set off little aftershocks.

Finally, when the tremors stopped, he lifted his head, eyes glowing, and kissed her full on the mouth. It was a different kiss this time, not so desperate but languorous and thorough, a reminder of where she'd just been and a promise of more to come.

Her body was so limp she didn't think more was possible, until he stroked her bare breast and nudged her knees apart so he could settle between her legs.

Impossible it might be, yet Miranda felt a jolt of shocking pleasure arc between her breast and the apex of her thighs where his arousal rested. Her hips tilted, stroking his engorged flesh. What he'd done before felt fantastic but this...

'I can't wait any longer.'

His voice was rough, almost unrecognisable as he reached between them, the tendons in his neck standing proud and his high-cut cheekbones more pronounced.

Miranda felt a weight between her thighs.

'I need to tell you something,' she blurted, because suddenly it was important he knew. He'd given her such delight she needed to warn him not to expect too much in return.

Zamir stiffened, his body turning to stone under her hands. 'You've changed your mind?'

'No!' How could he think that? She'd never experienced ecstasy like that and every instinct told her there was more, as good if not better, to come. She cleared her throat. 'It's just that I haven't done this before. I might disappoint you.'

His eyes snapped wide. 'You said—'

'I misled you. I didn't want to admit I don't have any experience when you probably have so much. I wanted to…'

'Tease me?'

'No.' She paused. 'I wanted not to seem vulnerable or weak. I've been out of my depth since we met and I wanted, for once, to be your equal in something.'

That made her sound sad and pathetic. A couple of days ago she'd never have admitted it but after what had just happened, her defences were shattered. She wanted him to understand.

But instead of accepting her warning, Zamir reared back as if stung. Her heart plummeted. Had she destroyed the moment?

'When you say no experience, you mean *no* experience?'

Miranda scrabbled to sit up, pulling her bodice over her heaving breasts. 'I've been kissed.' He raised his eyebrows and she shrugged. 'But I've never had sex.'

Zamir scrubbed a hand over his face. 'In that case we'd better not—'

'No!' In a flurry of fabric she closed the space between them, one hand clutching his bulging biceps. 'Don't say we have to stop. Just because I'm a virgin doesn't mean I can't learn.'

'Stop?' His nostrils flared and he shook his head as he stroked her cheek, his fingers trailing from there to her bare breast, revealed by her now-drooping bodice, making her shiver. 'You credit me with too many scruples. I was just going to suggest we move to the bedroom. Your first time shouldn't be on a sofa.'

Relief made her laugh. 'Is that a rule? You can't take my virginity on a sofa?'

His mouth ticked up at the corners in that bare hint of a grin that turned her insides to mush. 'Not a rule. I just think it better that you're comfortable.'

'I'm comfortable here.'

Miranda had an unreasoning fear that if they stopped long enough to move to another room he'd change his mind. It made no sense but her mind wasn't functioning on logic.

She stroked her hand up his arm, her other hand reaching for his groin and that proud erection that so fascinated her. But Zamir grabbed her wrist, preventing her reaching her goal.

'Teach me, Zamir.' She leaned close, feathering a kiss to the corner of his mouth then across to his neck, remembering the shatteringly decadent sensation he'd elicited when he'd caressed her there. 'Show me.'

She grazed her teeth at a spot just below his ear and he shuddered, his big body trembling at her touch.

How strange and wonderful to feel such power. She could get used to it. Except she didn't want power over Zamir. She wanted them together.

Miranda lifted her head and met eyes glazed with desire. His large hands cupped her breasts, his touch firm yet so gentle she felt something dissolve inside. As if a too-tight knot unravelled. She arched, pushing her breasts into his hands, revelling in the febrile heat she read in his eyes as much as the delicious sensations.

He spoke softly. 'You're a headstrong woman.'

'And you like it.'

It was only as she heard the words that she realised they were true. There was nothing but desire and approval in his expression. No matter how they'd argued, he'd never loathed her feistiness the way her uncle did.

'Perhaps I do.' He rolled her nipples between his fingers and she gasped at the shock of delight that arced from his touch straight to her core. 'Now stop talking and straddle me.'

'Straddle?'

Her brain seemed to have slowed and Zamir finally betrayed impatience by grabbing her hips and lifting her bodily over him. She knelt, one knee on either side of his thighs, facing him, her long skirts bundled up around her waist.

She shifted her weight as something warm and solid brushed her inner thigh. Her breath snared as she realised what it was.

'Absolutely sure?'

Miranda nodded, steadying herself on those broad straight shoulders as he reached beneath the crumpled dress. 'What now?'

Zamir's smile was tight, as if he were in pain. She wanted to query that but kept quiet. There was something she wanted more. She moved her knees wider and felt the head of his erection stroke her again.

'Just sink down, slowly.'

Taking a fortifying breath, because despite everything she *was* a little nervous, she lowered herself, pausing as his flesh notched against her entrance.

Miranda recalled the size of his arousal, perfectly in keeping with the size of the man, but significantly larger than she'd expected. But she wanted this, wanted him, so much, even the prospect of a little pain didn't daunt her.

Biting the corner of her mouth in concentration, she sank down then paused.

'Oh!'

Nothing had prepared her for the strange feeling of fullness as their bodies merged.

'It hurts?' Zamir leaned forward and nuzzled her breast, kissing and grazing it gently with his teeth, making her shudder and her eyes close. Internal muscles softened and eased and without further thought she slipped down further and further until her breath disappeared because it felt as if they'd truly become one. She felt the joining not only in her pelvis but higher, in her chest where her heart quickened and her lungs faltered for a moment at the enormity of this miracle.

'Miranda. Does it hurt?'

She shook her head. 'It just feels...'

She opened her eyes and met his, so close he should be blurry, yet somehow he wasn't. She saw him clearly. The man, not the Sheikh. The lover who'd already brought her such bliss.

Miranda didn't have words. Instead she leaned in and kissed him full on the mouth with gratitude and joy. With all the pent-up yearning she'd battled. With the tattered wreckage of the fear and doubt she'd clung to and which he'd vanquished with his simple, honest praise, turning her tormenting thoughts inside out and offering her a bright new reality.

She couldn't name her emotions as she offered and he accepted, her hands now cupping his face, his arms wrapped tight around her back as if he couldn't bear any distance between them.

She devoured his mouth and he let her, then devoured her right back.

And when he shifted beneath her, bumping his hips so she rode higher, she gasped. For deep as he was, that nudged a spot that hummed in pure delight.

'Lift up,' he urged against her mouth and his hands slid to her hips, grasping and gently drawing her higher till she wanted to protest because it felt like withdrawal. Except then, with a little downward pressure, he had her sinking so they fitted more snugly than ever.

Miranda felt her eyes widen as other parts of her body cheered in awed delight.

Now she understood.

Leaning in to kiss him deeply, she rose again then let gravity do its work, creating more glorious friction as they locked together once more.

This time Zamir's fingers clamped tight at her hips and he groaned in the back of his throat. She tasted the sound on her tongue, rough and delicious, and wanted more.

She wanted to give him the joy he'd given her.

Eagerly she rose and fell, slowly then faster, excitement feeding off his obvious pleasure.

Zamir's grip turned harder but she loved that, feeling he teetered on the edge of the same ecstasy he'd given her. Meanwhile the friction between their bodies and the amazing feeling of oneness pushed her on. She twisted her hips, learning how to milk pleasure from each movement.

Something changed. The tempo. Zamir's breathing. And Miranda's excitement rose. She felt tremors course through his body and realised he was close to climax. The idea was incredibly arousing, though she knew this time was for him, not her.

Then Zamir slid his hands from her hips, leaving her totally in control. He cupped her breast and leaned forward to take her nipple in his mouth and suck. Instantly she faltered, shuddering as a bolt of lightning hit her.

She'd just found her rhythm again when his hand slid under her dress, warm against her abdomen, thumb pressing down on that most sensitive spot in her whole body.

Miranda's eyes widened. Her body jerked and she felt an answering throb from Zamir.

That was all it took to send her careering out of control, riding him with a desperate, ungainly eagerness that jolted them together and turned their smooth union into a jerky, ecstatic race to rapture.

CHAPTER TWELVE

'MORE, ZAMIR. MORE, PLEASE!'

In the pre-dawn quiet Miranda's voice was a raw gasp, barely audible over the surge of blood in his ears. But he saw her mouth form the words, her lips reddened from passion. Her short nails dug into his flesh and her strong, supple legs encircled his hips, caging him.

As if he wanted to be anywhere but here!

Then thought was beyond him. There was just Miranda convulsing in pleasure, destroying the last of his stamina and drawing him to triumphant climax.

He buried his face against the curve of her neck, drawing in the deep floral and female scent of her while he spilled himself gratefully into velvety warmth. Each climax with her seemed more phenomenal than the last.

Ages later he came to himself enough to think of his weight bearing down on her so, wrapping her in his arms, he rolled onto his back so she lay limp above him, their panting breaths in unison.

He had no perception of time. The world comprised just himself and Miranda. He knew hours had passed. They'd slept a little and, after that first time, they'd bathed in the sunken tub of gold-veined marble that he'd never used because a quick shower was more efficient.

Now he didn't care about efficient. He luxuriated in the physical senses.

Miranda had been a revelation. Her disarming honesty had cut past his pride. She'd revealed doubts and insecurities that surprised him and made him want to protect her, though he suspected she wouldn't accept that. She was so determinedly independent.

And brave. He'd never forget her expression when he'd taken her virginity. How she'd paused, face twisted in discomfort if not pain, nails biting his flesh.

He'd been ready to withdraw, loath to hurt her. But she'd taken stock then simply continued, trusting him to make it good for her. It had been typical of her gallant determination and made him even more committed to making her first time memorable for all the best reasons.

Significantly though, Miranda had also revealed another side to *him*. A pleasure-seeker, determined to wrest every last drop of sensual pleasure from their bodies.

Zamir enjoyed sex but tonight had been different. He felt more…engaged. The climaxes had been more acute, his delight in her arousal an end in itself. He'd given her orgasms, not just because he was a considerate lover, but because her incandescent joy was his too.

There was something different about Miranda.

Something portentous about their coming together.

Instinctively, he shied from the idea, searching for logic to explain the inexplicable.

It's because she was a virgin.

He'd wanted to ensure this was good for her too.

And because she's your wife. You have a vested interest in keeping her happy.

Except this was more than keeping a sexual partner happy.

In the past, when the senses were sated, Zamir had had no difficulty pulling away. He'd chosen partners who wanted short affairs not emotional connection.

Yet all night, after each climax, instead of craving the usual solace of privacy, Zamir had wanted Miranda in his arms. Their limbs tangled together, as if he cherished her closeness as much as the sex they'd shared.

Gently he stroked her back and she snuggled against his chest. Zamir felt such deep satisfaction at having her here, sprawled boneless above him, that it should shock him. But he'd become inured to surprises where Miranda was concerned.

After that first time he'd decided to hold back for the rest of the night. She was unused to sex and he was a big man. He would let her sleep undisturbed the rest of the night.

For once he couldn't follow through on his decision. The urges of his body undermined his brain.

It was as if he had no control. When they'd left the bath he'd mentioned returning her to her room, because if they slept in separate rooms his resolve wouldn't be so tested. She'd looked at him with huge silvery eyes and his good intentions had dissolved.

He couldn't help but be pleased that his bride enjoyed sex so much. Her enthusiasm belied her inexperience and she learned fast. Already she was frighteningly effective at seducing him. She'd be positively dangerous when she realised the extent of her power.

Zamir frowned. He wasn't afraid of a sexually strong woman. In fact, the idea stirred a libido that should be dormant after their recent activities.

Yet he was unsettled.

Since the age of ten, his life had followed a strict reg-
imen. Every hour accounted for and used to best effect.
He rarely took time off and had never been tempted to
while away a day in bed.

He was sorely tempted now. In fact he was mentally
running through this morning's appointments, trying to
persuade himself they could be rescheduled.

Zamir wanted to stay with Miranda. Have a little
of the honeymoon that had been denied them because
there'd been too many important matters to deal with
when they returned from Aboussir. Because it was vital
his wife be accepted without question. That she slot-
ted into her role without raising too many eyebrows or
causing major scandal. Questions about her suitabil-
ity as Queen would reflect on him and on the planned
merger of nations.

Yet he found it hard to think about politics.

He wanted…his breath locked in his throat as he
realised what he wanted most was to be here with Miranda. He wanted to forget his obligations and carve
out time for private pleasure.

For sex, yes. But there was more too. He wanted to
take her riding at sunset on the coast. He could imagine
her grin as they galloped together along the wet sand
as the sun turned the water to fire.

He wanted to see her expression when he drove her
into the mountain town famed for its ancient houses
carved into the rocks. To the hot-air balloon festival
when hundreds of colourful balloons rose delicately in
the dawn light.

He'd take her into the desert to his favourite oasis,

just the two of them. He had a hunch she'd appreciate some of the things he loved about his country.

Since when did you expect or want a honeymoon?

Yours was always going to be a marriage of convenience.

Honeymoons are for people who believe in romance. Not royals with millions depending on them.

A chill wound its way from Zamir's prickling hairline, down his vertebrae and plunged into his belly.

He remembered his uncle's response when he'd begged to be allowed to play football with his friends. The kind but stern voice reminding him he had an obligation to his nation. To learn to be the best ruler he could. To put the nation's needs above his own. And never to forget that.

It had been drummed into him that duty must always come before personal feelings. It was one of the reasons he'd kept going, stoic through bereavement.

Was this, now, him forgetting his responsibilities? Letting emotion rule?

After twenty years of doing his royal duty, was he sliding into selfishness?

You're allowed time off. You're not a machine.

But the way he felt, he'd take an hour for himself and it would become three. A day would become a week. He had to put the brakes on while he still could. Because Miranda threatened to undermine the work ethic that was his core strength. Without it…

He couldn't allow that. He had to be strong, not let selfishness undermine him.

Gently he slid out from under Miranda, rolling her onto her side, and rose from the bed.

His worst fears were realised when he saw the time.

He'd noticed the strip of daylight edging the curtains but ignored it. Now he was late for his meetings.

A noise woke Miranda. She lay sprawled in a vast bed. Without opening her eyes she knew it was Zamir's. It smelled of him and of sex. She was boneless with a mixture of tiredness and exhilaration that felt close to heaven. The only thing that would make it better was Zamir.

She opened her eyes and there he was, emerging from the bathroom. He wore a charcoal suit and had just shaved.

She shivered voluptuously, remembering the exciting scrape of his bristly chin along her inner thigh and elsewhere.

Who'd known sex could be so wondrous?

Not just sex but sex with Zamir. Her insides twisted in excitement as their gazes locked. But instead of meeting a heavy-lidded look of sensual awareness, Miranda confronted a cool, unreadable scrutiny. Gone was the warmth, the beguiling invitation, the connection.

The man before her, with his flat mouth and pinched nostrils, reminded her of the haughty enemy she'd first met.

Instantly her lassitude disappeared as she scrabbled for the sheet, tucking it around herself as she sat up against the pillows.

Something flared in his eyes before he looked away. 'Sorry, I didn't mean to wake you. Stay here and rest. There's no need for you to get up, but I have business—'

'Wait!' Miranda didn't know what she was going to say, just that she wasn't ready for him to leave.

Fool. Can't you see he can't wait to get out of here?

If she'd needed anything to remind her that she was the novice when it came to sex, and he the expert, his attitude now proved it. She'd thought they'd shared something glorious and special. He couldn't wait to go. His precious business appealed more than her, now he'd had what he wanted.

Miranda swallowed and jutted her chin higher, striving to keep the hurt from her voice. 'At least tell me how to get back to my room. I don't fancy doing the morning-after walk of shame through the palace.'

That stopped him in his tracks. He turned to face her fully, frowning. 'There's no shame involved. We're husband and wife.'

Her eyes narrowed. 'But that's how this feels. Especially with you…' she waved one hand, searching for words '…dismissing me with a curt couple of words.'

Zamir's eyes widened and his hand went to his perfectly knotted tie. 'Dismissing you?'

He drew himself taller, shoulders back, chin angled proudly, sooty eyebrows forming a deep V, the image of superiority.

Then he shook his head and approached the bed. Gleaming eyes captured hers and again she felt that fizz of connection as if he only had to look at her and she was his. As if she had no pride.

Zamir sat beside her, his arm caging her body as he planted his palm beside her hip.

'I'm sorry, Miranda.' His voice was gravelly, his gaze searching. 'I wasn't thinking.'

His mouth turned down at the corners and his chest lifted on a deep sigh as he raked his hand through his hair. Predictably, it fell back in place perfectly. How did he do that? Miranda knew she looked rumpled while Zamir was as perfectly put together as ever.

He plucked her hand from the sheet, threading his fingers through hers. 'Dismissal was the last thing on my mind.' He paused. 'The trouble was I panicked.'

She'd never seen anyone more obviously in control.

'Panicked? I find that hard to believe.'

With her hand in his, his thumb stroking her palm and his gorgeous scent tantalising her nostrils, Miranda's voice sounded breathless rather than accusing.

'It's true.' He looked at their joined hands then pressed warm lips to her flesh, sending a shiver of reaction cascading through her weak frame.

He murmured something she didn't catch over the thunder of her blood. But she did hear him add, 'This is outside my experience.'

Miranda couldn't prevent a huff of laughter. 'Surely that's my line.'

Abruptly he looked up, amusement creating long dimples in his cheeks, his eyes alight and smile rueful. 'So it is. Though it doesn't feel like it. You undo me, Miranda.'

For a moment he looked as surprised as she felt. *She* undid *him*? Her pulse thudded wildly.

'I'm not used to being married. And before you say anything, of course that applies to us both. What I'm used to are short, discreet affairs away from the palace. My work and private life don't intermingle. I didn't know we were going to spend the night together. I have to work this morning.'

He flicked a glance at the expensive watch on his wrist. 'Instead of having the luxury to stay with you, I have a packed schedule. All important matters that need my personal attention. And I'm already half an hour late for my first meeting.'

'You'd rather spend the morning here with me?'

His look of astonishment spoke for itself. 'How can you doubt it?'

He lifted her hand, pressing it to his groin where she felt a now-familiar rigid length. Heat filled her and her fingers curled possessively.

Zamir wanted her. What had he said? That she undid him.

Relief flooded and that delicious feeling that they shared this attraction as equals. But it was short-lived as he gently pried her hand away.

'Not now.' His voice sounded thick and unfamiliar. 'I have an international trade delegation waiting for me. I can't insult them by being even later.'

This time when he spoke, Miranda saw what it cost him. She felt the fine tremor running through his big frame and the tension in his muscles.

'I came in from the bathroom and saw you awake and knew I had to leave straight away before I did something rash.'

Zamir leaned close, his free hand cupping her jaw, fingertips burrowing into her hair as he kissed her, deliberately, longingly, carnally.

That was all it took to blank Miranda's mind of doubt and indignation. She pressed herself against him, giving herself unstintingly, the floodgates of desire bursting open. She yanked his hand to her breast. Clasping it there, she arched into his touch. A deep growl vibrated from his throat, making her shiver with anticipation.

But too soon he pulled away, capturing both her hands in his and holding them tight. 'This was exactly what I was afraid of. I can't, Miranda. As much as I want to, I have responsibilities that I can't ignore.'

Miranda watched his face, the fleeting emotions, and fastened on the most extraordinary one.

Zamir had been afraid.

It was a common expression, but, combined with his behaviour, she realised he meant it.

She threatened his focus and his timetable. But watching him watch her, she was convinced he didn't say that lightly. She knew how important Zamir's duty was to him. Not for the ego trip but because he genuinely believed his work made a difference.

He'd been afraid she'd tempt him into forgetting that.

Had she that much power? The idea stunned her and she needed time to think it through.

While he needed to work.

'Then you're forgiven. You'd better go.'

His mouth twisted. 'That's the hell of it. I don't want to.'

He lifted her hand to his mouth and kissed her knuckles, sending a shiver of need through her. He only had to touch her and her willpower dissolved. That terrified her. 'You still need to tell me how to get back to my room.'

His smile wound a ribbon of heat around her. 'Didn't you know we have adjoining suites?' He nodded to a door on the far side of the room. 'That goes straight to your bedroom.'

'All this time you've been sleeping just a room away?'

He nodded. 'We *are* married, after all.'

Was it the way his voice dropped to a soft, suede note, or the lambent fire in his gaze that took her immediately back to last night's intimacies? She found herself breathless and dazzled.

Too dazzled. Zamir might have stunned her with his admission of momentary panic because he'd rather stay than attend his meetings. But that was nothing to Miranda's crazy thoughts. She still felt they'd shared something utterly unique and special. Yet logic decreed it was just her inexperience trying to transform physical bliss into something more momentous.

If she wasn't careful she'd read too much into simple sex. On learning their rooms were a mere wall apart, she'd even mentally applauded Zamir's patience in not trying to use their proximity to seduce her earlier. Some men would have.

As if she didn't have the right to abstain from sex if she chose!

But you don't want to abstain. You want Zamir, more even than before.

Last night had changed things. Changed *her*. She needed to regroup and think things through. As it was, she was only slowly coming to terms with the implications of what they'd shared.

'Before you go,' she began. 'We didn't use contraception.'

He nodded gravely. 'Yes. For the first time ever I realised that after the event. But there's no need to worry about an infection. I—'

'I was actually concerned about pregnancy.' She hadn't got as far as thinking about STDs.

He stilled. 'You don't want children?'

Had he simply assumed she would? Miranda wished she could read him better. Through the night it had felt as if they'd connected at such an elemental level that everything between them would simply fall into place, the way their bodies did. Clearly that wasn't so.

'I suppose I assumed I'd have children one day.'

She sat back, pulling her hands from his, realising abruptly how very convenient it would be for Zamir if last night left her pregnant. He'd married to secure the kingdom and, by his own admission, the succession.

Had that been part of the reason he'd wanted her?

'But I'm not ready for a child.' Panic made her voice strident. 'We don't know each other. Except physically. It would be a disaster.'

Again Zamir's expression turned inscrutable. But it wasn't foolproof, for Miranda read his thudding pulse and the tiny firming of his lips. He wasn't happy.

A second later he unfolded himself from the bed to stand, surveying her from his lofty height. 'Very well. I'll arrange a doctor's appointment today so you can consider contraception options and I'll get condoms for next time.' He paused. 'Assuming there'll be a next time?'

It was on the tip of her tongue to say no because she hated the sudden distance between them, and the feeling it was her fault. But she had no reason to feel guilty. Her stipulation was reasonable.

And what was the point pretending? He only had to touch her and she went up in flames.

'Yes,' she managed, her voice only a little hoarse. 'There'll be a next time.'

For a second they stared at each other, then, belying what she'd believed to be his annoyance, Zamir leaned down and kissed her on the mouth. Not hard but thoroughly, so thoroughly her head was spinning as he pulled back and straightened his tie while she slumped, boneless against the pillows.

'Rest now, Miranda. I'll cancel your lessons for this morning so you can catch up on sleep. You'll need it.'

CHAPTER THIRTEEN

THE NEXT FEW weeks Zamir struggled to get through his work. He kept zoning out, attention straying to his unpredictable, irresistible wife.

Miranda was more challenging than any politician or negotiator. She made him feel things he never had.

He wanted as he'd never wanted before. His continual need for her undermined his resolution to do his job.

Enough even to admit in an unguarded moment how he feared her ability to distract him. Zamir *never* admitted weakness. He'd learned that at his uncle's knee.

Yet though he and Miranda still needed to negotiate some things, he no longer felt they were on opposing sides.

He trusted her.

The more he understood her, the more he liked and appreciated her. He'd rather have her reckless courage and honesty than a bride who simply nodded and agreed with him.

Even if sometimes Miranda wrong-footed him and injured his pride. Like when they'd discussed contraception.

Zamir *never* forgot contraception. Except with her. When he realised, he'd allayed his guilt by telling himself they were married and a child was expected. It was only when she called him on it that he realised how thoughtless that was. He imagined how doubly trapped Miranda would feel if she got pregnant so early in their relationship. He couldn't do that to her while she still faced so many challenges. When she regretted being here.

Knowing that made him feel…wrong. Even if it was too late to end their marriage.

He remembered his parents' relationship. The distance between them and with their children. Zamir didn't want that for any children he might have. He wanted—he realised with sudden certainty—something different to his parents' arrangement.

He wanted children who were loved and knew it. He wanted to be more than a polite stranger to his wife.

Miranda had cut him off at the knees when she'd admitted to insecurities behind her bravado. And *still* she was one of the strongest people he knew.

He'd witnessed vulnerability, obviously rooted in childhood, which made her doubt herself. He'd been sickened that her family had tried to squash her spirit. It made him realise his actions had played into that past negativity.

Because of that Zamir was determined to give his wife the freedom to be herself, to blossom, despite the parameters of royal life. He'd started out needing a suitable queen. But now…

He wanted Miranda to be happy.

It was as simple and complex as that. How thoughtless had been his plan to acquire a wife. As if she'd be two-dimensional, without her own needs and frailties, desires and strengths. After years working with his uncle, listening to the people, arbitrating disputes, hearing their issues and devising solutions, how could he not have anticipated that?

He didn't have to choose between Miranda and his duty because he realised now they were bound together.

Now the man who'd spent two decades adhering to every dictate of royal expectation found himself looking for ways to ease that burden. Not because his wife was weak, but because it hurt to think of all that vibrancy and honesty muffled and unappreciated.

Because she hated formal lessons he'd reduced them and taught her himself in relaxed conversations during sunset rides or over a meal. Until, inevitably, they were distracted by their desire for each other. He ignored the voice of caution warning he was shifting his priorities because of her. For Zamir was assiduous in ensuring he didn't neglect his official duties.

His lack of concentration was at least partly due to lack of sleep. Their sex life grew better and better.

When he wasn't with Miranda, he was imagining how it would be when he was. Her silky skin, her rich, enticing scent, her slender yet strong body matching his, wringing desperate responses that drained him, leaving him bereft of any pretence that he controlled this situation.

On the outside he might look like the man he'd always been but inside he felt different.

His increasing awareness of Miranda's issues made him think more carefully about other things. He found himself revisiting earlier judgements, listening harder to petitioners, and urging his staff to find more innovative answers to complex social problems. Because one size didn't fit everyone. Over the years he and his uncle had introduced useful reforms. But had they gone far enough? Had they been effective and inclusive for everyone? Had there been people left out, distanced and excluded?

Zamir left his last meeting but instead of returning to his office, on impulse took the corridor that led to the back of the palace.

That impulse being the need to see Miranda. He stifled the stern voice of conscience telling him he had a lot of work yet to do.

Surely checking on this new social initiative counted as work? Miranda had been helping at horse-riding sessions for people with disabilities. Each time she'd returned glowing and full of enthusiasm. Instead of complaining about the staff who accompanied her whenever she left the palace, she'd roped some of them into helping.

The change in her, having a purpose again, something she believed in, made him swell with pride and admiration. She seemed more confident too, attending several official functions with him.

Which was why, after she'd presented a persuasive case, Zamir had given qualified approval to a new project here at the palace. A pilot programme working with teenagers who'd skirted the edge of the legal system and who were likely to get into more trouble.

Zamir applauded a scheme to keep youngsters from incarceration and hopefully set them on a better path. Yet he'd wanted to bar Miranda's personal involvement with potentially dangerous young men.

There was that protective instinct kicking in.

He'd wrestled with his conscience, discussed the programme with Miranda and others, including expert youth workers, and finally decided not to interfere. It seemed she was an expert too, having worked with a similar programme at her stepfather's ranch.

His wife was full of surprises. She'd won over Zamir's old-fashioned stable master and not merely with her riding skills. She'd helped several horses recuperate from injury with what the older man called magic hands. She, shrugging, said it was a combination of massage and osteopathy.

His impressed stable master said she'd be able to name her own salary at any professional stable.

Practical, eager to help and with a social conscience yet no sense of entitlement or self-importance. Miranda might at first glance not fit the traditional idea of a queen. Yet she was impressive in so many ways.

The pilot programme had begun three days ago in the royal stables and Zamir had deliberately stayed away, giving those involved space. Besides, Miranda enthusiastically updated him each evening and Hassan was on hand to ensure there were no problems.

'I wondered how long you'd manage to stay away.'

Hassan's softly spoken words stopped him in the shaded colonnade opposite the stables.

Zamir raised an eyebrow. 'The trouble with having a head of security who's known you for years is they think they can read your mind.'

Hassan smiled. He nodded to where several horses stood patiently. 'I had my doubts about this but I'm beginning to wonder if there might be something in it. A couple of the boys stop their tough-guy posturing as soon as they're around the animals. And most pay attention even if they pretend not to.'

They watched in silence as Miranda and two others went up and down the line, murmuring advice and watching as young men undid the girths and lifted off saddles.

At the end of the row one wiry youth had difficulty. He said something and Miranda moved in close to assist. Suddenly the youth lunged, making a grab for her breast.

Zamir was crossing the courtyard at a run when Hassan's hand on his arm stopped him. 'Wait. Watch.'

Miranda didn't even flinch. In what felt like slow motion, Zamir saw her reach for the guy's wrist as she seemed to buckle at the knees, drawing him off balance as she kicked out. A moment later he was flat on the ground and she was standing, looking remarkably unruffled.

A gangly youth hurried to her side, hands clenching, but she shook her head and directed him back to his horse.

'She knows what she's doing.' Hassan sounded admiring. 'I saw her in action the first day. She has obviously faced that or worse before. I might borrow her to teach my team some moves.' He chuckled.

Zamir wasn't amused. He hated the idea of Miranda needing to defend herself. The idea of anyone touching her.

'That kid's out of the programme right now,' he growled, moving forward.

'You think she'll thank you for that?' That stopped Zamir. Reluctantly he turned and met Hassan's stare. 'You'll undermine her authority if you interfere.'

Zamir drew a shuddering breath that didn't fill his lungs. Instinct wrestled with logic. He watched the kid get to his feet, shoulders hunched and, after a quick look around, reach for the horse's girth.

It went against everything Zamir had been taught, everything he was, not to intervene. He ruled and protected, and punished too. He defended the defenceless.

But Miranda wasn't defenceless. She was capable. If he barged in now...

He knew from her own words that she felt out of her depth in Qu'sil, with little autonomy and no control. She'd taken her first steps to establishing both friendships and purpose through the equestrian group. He couldn't stop something so important to her.

More, he owed Miranda his support. She'd been an unwilling bride yet she'd been at his side publicly several times, edgy but valiantly determined to appear as a supportive spouse. She'd been so successful he'd almost believed the image of a contented, gracious wife.

Reluctantly he retreated into the shadows to lean, jaw gritted and arms folded, against the wall. The problem was this was no hypothetical issue. It was *personal*.

He waited till the session ended. A vehicle took the kids away and the staff dissipated, their working day over. Miranda headed into the stable and Zamir followed.

He found her in one of the small rooms at the far end of the now-deserted building, where records and supplies were stored. She perched on a stool, writing up notes at a high bench. A spill of lamplight revealed rich colour in her dark hair.

Zamir leaned against the door jamb. 'How did it go?'

She looked up, eyes lighting, and he had to shove his hands in his pockets rather than reach for her.

'I didn't expect to see you.' She sounded breathless,

pleased, which made his own breath seize. 'I thought you had meetings.'

'They finished early.' Because he'd rushed through business, fired by his urgency to be with her.

'It went well. It's early days but some of them are responding positively and they're all still participating. I think we're winning their trust slowly. There's one—'

'Who's causing trouble?'

She pushed her chair back from the desk. 'I was going to say, there's one who has really taken to this. He's even volunteered to help a local vet clinic.' She paused. 'What made you think there was trouble?'

'I was here earlier.' Zamir couldn't prevent his harsh tone as the words emerged through gritted teeth.

Miranda's eyes narrowed and she sat straighter. 'Why bother asking how it went if you were spying on me?'

'Not spying! I just wanted to see you. Then that kid assaulted you.'

Wood shrieked against tiles as she shoved the stool back, rising so abruptly it tumbled to the floor. She faced him, chest rising sharply on each quick breath, her face flushed and eyes brilliant.

'*Tried* to assault me. He didn't succeed. He was testing, seeing how far he could push.'

Zamir made himself pause before replying. 'Attempted assault is a crime too.'

Miranda bustled closer, her breath feathering his chin. 'You wouldn't! What do you think would happen to the programme if you brought in the police?'

'It's your safety I'm worried about.' Zamir couldn't eradicate the image of that lout reaching for Miranda.

'You think I can't take care of myself? I'm not even

alone! As well as the other volunteers your security guys are always on hand, trying to look inconspicuous.'

Zamir wrestled with the need to take charge and remove any threat. 'I'd like to see him dropped from the programme.' Miranda was already opening her mouth to argue when he added, 'But I understand your perspective. You can look after yourself and you've taken safety precautions.' He paused. 'If there's a chance this pilot programme can work, it's too important to be shut down before it gets started.'

For only the second time, he saw her speechless. Yet Zamir felt no victory, for the blood still coursed hot and angry in his arteries at the effort of restraint.

Finally she spoke. 'You mean it? You're not going to interfere?'

'I *want* to teach that kid a quick, unforgettable lesson in respect, then eject him from the programme.' Zamir slowly shook his head, pushing down the savage urge for violent reprisal. 'But I won't. If *you* promise to be careful and never be alone with him. And cut him loose if he tries anything like that again.'

'I promise.' Her words were soft.

'Good.' He cleared his throat, feeling a strange, febrile heat as if the emotion in her silvery eyes dug under his skin, which drew too tight. At the same time his lungs atrophied, forgetting for a second how to work.

'You trust me.'

Zamir wasn't sure if her whispered words were a statement or a question.

He nodded. Of course he trusted her. She was obstinate and impulsive but generous and truthful.

She made him feel things he had no name for. No experience of. She made him feel…too much.

But she was *here*, *his*, and there was no going back.

'I trust you, Miranda. And I don't want you hurt.'

Her hands landed on his chest, one palm above his hammering heart, and even that felt wonderful. He'd been scared, he realised, watching her defend herself, his heart in his mouth and a roar of bloodlust in his ears.

Suddenly his arms were around her, hauling her close. Something huge and powerful shuddered through him as he buried his face in her hair and inhaled the scent of woman, jasmine and horse. The perfect combination of alluring and down-to-earth, so typical of his wife.

Instead of questioning or debating, she sank against him, her arms slipping around him and holding tight.

A wave of something crashed through him. Relief. Satisfaction. A feeling of homecoming. As if he belonged here in this windowless room instead of in the palace's lavish, royal suite.

As if none of the accoutrements of power mattered. Just Miranda, safe in his arms.

'I want you,' he groaned, drawing her up against him. *Needed her.*

But that was better unsaid. After their first night together he'd betrayed his desperate hunger for her and part of him, the part that had trained most of his life to become ruler, warned it was a mistake to reveal such weakness.

'Good.' Her voice was muffled against his shirt collar. 'I want you too.'

Miranda tilted her head and there it was again, that earth-moving shudder as grey eyes met his and light lanced through his body like lightning racing to earth. It left him trembling with anticipation.

Stepping further into the room, he kicked the door shut, lifting her off her feet, and sat her on the sturdy bench.

Now they were almost eye to eye and Zamir recognised excitement blazing in her features. All the emotion he'd battled to hold in fought for release. Maybe she felt the same. His wife was no milk-and-water miss, submissive and serene. She was feisty, emotional, strong, and their passion always blazed stronger after argument.

'Touch me,' he ordered, uncaring that his gruff tone betrayed him.

Her smile was a siren's as she reached up to undo his tie. That wasn't what he'd had in mind but her hands were deft, already undoing his shirt buttons so she could lean to press her lips against bare skin.

He clutched her to him, his sigh of relief audible. Then her quick hands moved under his jacket lapels, pushing the fabric over his shoulders, and he released her for long enough to shrug free.

'Nice as that is, it's not what I meant.'

He placed his hands around her hips and tugged her close so her knees widened around him. His stirring erection pressed against that sweet spot between her thighs. Syrupy heat thickened his blood as he bucked forward, eyes closing for a moment at how good that felt.

'Did you mean this?'

Her voice was as husky as his as she insinuated one hand between them, fingers curling around his length. Zamir surged into her hold, the air dragging from his mouth.

'More.'

'You're so bossy.' Yet her eyes danced as she reached for his belt. 'But I'll forgive you this time.'

Tension pulled his skin tight as the ends of the belt fell and she undid his trousers. 'Because you want me too, don't you?'

She paused for the tiniest moment and Zamir drew the tension of waiting deep inside. He craved her touch but there was something else he needed. Then she gave it to him.

'I do,' she whispered as if her throat had tightened too. 'I want you inside me.'

His breath shuddered out and he bit down hard on his molars, searching for the control he needed not to spill himself in her warm hand.

Zamir grabbed her wrists, capturing them in one hand as he reached into his pocket before his trousers slid low. His eyes held hers as he tore the packet with his teeth, watching the flare of excitement in her stare. That notched up his own arousal to impossible levels. His hand shook as he fumbled the condom.

'I could do that for you.' She licked her lips as she looked down and he throbbed hard in anticipation.

'Not this time.'

He was too close. In fact, it would be better if he took care of her first in case he couldn't hold on.

He was so distracted he barely noticed her hands slide from his hold. In a few swift movements she'd pulled off her boots, dropping them to the floor, then undone her zip, lifting her hips to shimmy out of her trousers and underwear.

Zamir's chest ached as she opened her legs.

She was beautiful all over. Yet when he managed to

pull his attention up to her face he thought he caught a flicker of doubt. How could that be?

'You're gorgeous.' His throat was so raw she'd have to be a lip-reader to understand his words. Yet her slow-growing smile said she got the idea.

Condom on, he teased the downy hair between her thighs, arrowing down to that sweet, fleshy nub and watched her mouth open in a gasp of excitement as she rubbed against his touch.

The sight of her pleasure was addictive. The diamond-bright glint of her eyes, the forward thrust of her breasts as she arched her back, hands on the bench, the restless circling of her hips. His fingers were slick and he smelled that rich, earthy scent of feminine arousal.

Her breathing sharpened, her movements quickening and she was the most magnificent being he'd ever seen.

Then one small, capable hand encircled him as she wrapped her legs around his hips.

Zamir was only human and Miranda was irresistible.

What happened next came without conscious thought. It was as inevitable and as beautiful as sunrise over the desert. They came together so easily, so perfectly, it felt like destiny.

And pleasure. Instant, all-engulfing pleasure.

So tight and fast it rose like a sandstorm, blotting out the world and leaving the pair of them, gasping, juddering, caught on a point between astonishment and bliss until, hoarse cries curling together in the still room, they collapsed, holding tight as the world tilted and changed for ever.

CHAPTER FOURTEEN

'SADIA! IT'S WONDERFUL to hear from you. I've tried and tried but—'

'It's a relief to hear your voice too! I only just got access to a phone.' Miranda's cousin sounded different, her voice tight. 'I'm sorry. I've been frantic to find out how you are but couldn't get any news. My father took my phone and I haven't been allowed out.'

'Not allowed? What about your classes?' Sadia was a schoolteacher.

'No teaching. I've been under house arrest. Father brought in security guards for the wedding...' Her voice petered out. 'When the marriage didn't go ahead, he kept them on to guard *me*. I've never seen him so furious, ranting about me dishonouring the family and the nation. But,' she said in a firmer voice, 'he's more worried about missed opportunities because he's not father to a queen.'

'Oh, Sadia. We knew he'd be furious, but I never thought he'd lock you up.'

Miranda slumped onto a deeply cushioned window seat, staring at the manicured garden courtyard beyond the private pool. But in her mind's eye it was her uncle's house she saw, with its high walls and beautifully decorative but impenetrable metalwork over the windows.

The only way out, when the house was locked up, was over the roof. Miranda had gone that way herself last time she'd fallen foul of her uncle's temper. But she couldn't imagine decorous Sadia doing that.

'*I'm* all right. *I* wasn't the one forced into marriage.' Sadia's voice wobbled. 'That's all my fault. And I feel guilty too because it's worked out well for me. Mother ended up going to the Sheikh and with his backing I'm moving out of home into an apartment near the school.'

That was what Sadia had wanted for ages, but hadn't been able to push the point with her father.

'That's excellent news,' Miranda said, though she could guess at the emotional price her cousin paid for that freedom.

'Enough about me. How about you? I've been so worried, not knowing how you are.'

'Actually, I'm good. Far better than I'd imagined, though life here is a little different from working in South America.' She laughed reassuringly.

'Oh, Mira. Don't put on a brave face for me. I know what you're going through, or can at least imagine it. Remember, I was the one promised in marriage. Are you really okay?'

Her cousin always had been a worrier. 'More than okay. I'm very good.'

It was true. Life here wasn't what she'd planned, but then she'd never been a great planner. She'd fallen into a career by following her passion.

If anyone had told her she could find happiness in a palace, regularly appearing at formal events and married to a man she didn't know, she'd never have believed them.

But she did know Zamir. And what she knew she liked.

More than liked.

Miranda drew her knees up to her chest and wrapped her free arm around her legs, hugging tight the feelings that had been swelling inside her for weeks now. She wasn't just in lust with her husband. She admired him, liked being with him.

'It's very courageous of you....'

'Not courageous at all. Life here is easy and I get to do a lot of things I want as well as some things I'd rather not, but then that's life, isn't it?'

She was gradually getting used to being the centre of attention when she appeared in public but she doubted she'd ever get completely used to it. She fared better in informal situations but at least she could hold her own now, after Zamir had spent so much time helping her.

She'd even got used to the minders who accompanied her outside the palace, learning that instead of being disapproving spies they actually had her well-being at heart. Her new assistant was a mine of useful information and wasn't stuffy or formal.

Even dressing up in glamorous clothes could be fun now she'd taken her husband's advice to wear what made her feel good. Her wardrobe had been chosen or made specifically to suit her, so she didn't need to fear appearing as a frump. But what had really overcome her doubts had been Zamir's reaction. Again and again as he took in her appearance, ready for some official function, she read his approval. More than that, blatant desire.

His admiration was more effective than any mirror or well-meant compliment. He made her feel beautiful.

'But it's such an enormous change. Being hemmed in by all that royal protocol and ceremony. And then there's Zamir with his air of authority, his...*certainty*. Don't you find it stifling?'

On the contrary, Miranda found it exciting. Energising. Arousing.

You have a one-track mind.

'We have our disagreements,' she said carefully, 'but we get on well.'

Even disagreements could be fun. Miranda's family had accused her of being impulsive and emotional but she'd discovered an upside to being passionate about things she cared about. Like not being bulldozed into things she didn't want, or like the success of her riding and rehabilitation programmes.

Zamir took her passion in his stride, meeting it with an enthusiasm of his own, never dismissing her views. They debated politics, negotiated her role, sometimes argued, and she'd never felt more alive. More appreciated and valued. She loved the way he was always ready to meet passion with passion.

It was a heady thing, she'd discovered, being wife to Zamir of Qu'sil.

'I see.' Sadia sounded doubtful.

It was Miranda's turn to interrogate. 'I know you didn't want to marry him. But you said he was respectful if distant.' Which was natural between strangers. Knowing Zamir as she did, she saw past his reserve to the admirable, serious man who worked conscientiously for others. 'But there must have been more to it than that.' Sadia had been so panicked she hadn't been totally coherent.

Her cousin was silent for a long time. When she spoke again her voice was flat. 'I was scared about not having a say about marrying. Scared I wouldn't cope with everyone's expectations, especially in public.' Her voice dropped. 'Worried too because Zamir is such a determined, powerful man and you know I've never been able to stand up for myself.'

Miranda's mouth flattened. Sadia had been so cowed, growing up with a tyrannical father. Even now she carried the scars, the lack of confidence, and they skewed her perspective.

Had Miranda's initial view of Zamir been skewed too for the same reason? Of course it had.

'There's a difference between a powerful, determined man, doing his best for his people, like Zamir, and a small-minded despot who gets his kicks from ordering his family around and belittling anybody in the least different.'

That was why her uncle had never approved of her. She hadn't conformed even as a child. Not out of wilful disobedience but because she had an adventurous, questioning disposition, strengthened by early exposure to different cultures and places. She'd never fitted the narrow confines of his petty tyranny. Not because she was intrinsically bad or deficient, but because he didn't have the generosity or wisdom to accept difference.

'Zamir acted for the good of the nation, both nations. And yes, I didn't like marrying a total stranger. But you know what? He's the most decent, honourable, kind man.' Her throat tightened as her chest swelled. 'The only downside is that he's about to be crowned

King and that whole royal thing is still a challenge for me, though I'm getting better at it.'

She paused, swallowing hard. 'He's gone out of his way to help me and make life here a pleasure.'

Not just with learning to be royal, but introducing her to people who were fast becoming friends. Giving her leeway to pursue her charitable interests which, while laudable, didn't fit neatly with royal tradition. Trusting her to do them well. And all the while making her feel stronger, more valued, more special.

Then there was his tenderness, his laughter, the way his eyes shone when he looked at her, as if she were as mesmerising as a star-studded desert night.

Her breath hitched. Zamir's touch, from the casual brush of his hand against hers as they entered a formal reception, to the thrilling carnality of his lovemaking, was more powerful than anything she'd known. More wonderful.

'You like him. Really like him. I'm so glad!'

Miranda shifted against the cushions, staring at the still water in their private swimming pool. Just a few nights ago they'd made love there. Even on the edge of the city and at the heart of the vast, sprawling palace, it had felt as if they were the only two people in the world and that together they'd created magic.

Afterwards he'd cradled her as she lay blinking at the stars, wondering at the bliss that seemed to grow stronger and last longer whenever they came together.

Instead of falling asleep or turning away after his climax, Zamir had told her stories about the stars. Old tales about how they got their names, what they meant, and how to use them when navigating through the desert.

He'd answered every question then laughed with her

when she concocted her own alternative story about starry horses and riders racing across the velvet darkness. Laughed *with* her, not *at* her.

'Yes.' Miranda cleared her throat. 'I like him very much. You will too when you get to know him.'

The fact was, Miranda didn't just like him.

She loved him.

Her pulse beat high in her throat and her breathing grew shallow with the realisation. She'd always been impulsive, but falling in love in just a few weeks...

Not a few weeks.

Even that first day when she'd loathed him, there'd been something about Zamir that drew her. Something powerfully magnetic, an undercurrent of excitement and awareness at the most visceral level that called to her.

An excitement she felt now, thinking about him.

It was as if, without knowing his character or his kindness, she'd sensed them.

Why else would she have meekly stayed here in the palace that first night instead of sneaking out under cover of darkness and heading for the border? Yes, she'd been a prisoner but she hadn't even tried to escape, because deep down she'd been too intrigued by her captor.

Miranda blinked and the bright greens, blues and whites outside shifted, as if moving in a giant kaleidoscope, settling into a new, glorious pattern.

'I'm pleased he's good to you, Mira. You deserve that.' Sadia paused. 'It's in his interests to ensure you adapt to life there. He needs a content wife who will play her part well in public. But you know that. You understand it's not personal. You won't break your heart over him.'

Miranda ended the call soon after that. Her initial

elation at talking with Sadia had morphed into something else. Something horrible. Worse than her outrage when her cousin compared Zamir with Miranda's uncle.

Sadia was trying to be sensible, even kind. What she said about Zamir's interest in her being happy was logical.

Yet it felt wrong.

Miranda had wanted to protest that her husband wasn't simply being pragmatic. His actions weren't all carefully calculated for the good of his position.

She wanted to rant that Zamir cared about her.

That, at least, was true. Zamir *did* care. He *was* kind as well as practical.

But had she read too much into his kindness?

Had the beautiful gleam in his eyes when he looked at her been just a reflection of her own dazzled excitement? Was she imagining what she wanted to see rather than what was really there? Was she attributing feelings to him because her own lonely heart had locked on him?

The sad truth was that her heart had imprinted on him, like an orphaned baby animal imprinting on the first living being to show it affection.

Miranda had known love as a child but after her father died her mother's love seemed tainted with disappointment. Zamir was the first person since her dad, and, to a degree, Matias, to accept her as she was, with her faults, strengths, and idiosyncrasies. The first to make her feel valued and valuable.

To make her feel loved.

Was that, as Sadia warned, an illusion? A tactic to win her over? No, Zamir never lied to her. He wouldn't stoop so low He'd never mentioned love. *She* was the one who'd extrapolated.

If he felt…more for her, he'd have said. He wasn't a man given to self-doubt or hesitation. He was a man who knew about love. It was there in his voice when he spoke about his siblings, his sister studying dry land agriculture and his brother making documentaries. His affection for them was clear.

Surely if he felt the same way she did, he'd tell her? *Of course he would. Zamir has nothing to hide.*

Miranda doubled over, arms wrapped tight around her middle to hold in welling pain. But nothing could keep it back. It leaked out, growing stronger by the second.

She was in love with her husband.

A decent, kind man who tried to make her situation as easy as possible. A man who respected her but didn't love her.

Her stomach heaved and perspiration prickled her forehead. She felt she was going to be sick. But her ailment wasn't physical. She wished it were.

Dry-eyed, stomach churning, heart aching, she stared at the glittering water of their private swimming pool. She'd given herself to him there with love.

He'd given her joy and easy companionship. He had the gift of making her feel important though the fact was that she, as an individual, wasn't. He'd needed to marry a woman from her country, her family, and he had. That was the bare, brutal truth she'd forgotten in these last weeks.

Zamir was simply pragmatist enough to want a content spouse. He'd told her that for generations his family's marriages had been arranged for dynastic reasons, not love.

She was the only one foolish enough to dream of love.

The truth was so simple, she was astounded she hadn't recognised it sooner.

Miranda shot to her feet, yanking off her couture clothes as she hurried to her dressing room.

Soon after, in jeans, boots and a plain shirt, she was riding Chico, trying to ease the hurt that seemed too big for her body.

It didn't work. When finally they returned to the stables, exhausted, the pain had solidified into a hard ache in the pit of her stomach.

The only thing she'd achieved was the realisation she couldn't live the rest of her life this way. Miranda's self-esteem had taken a battering for too many years, to the extent that her self-doubts had made her second-guess her instincts.

For most of her life she'd been second best. Not wanted or chosen for herself but out of duty. Her husband had married her as a convenient replacement for the woman he really wanted.

Her bitter laugh made Chico turn and nuzzle her questioningly as she brushed his steaming body. She leaned against his solid shoulder, murmuring reassurances as she breathed in his comforting equine smell.

'What am I going to do, Chico? This can't go on.'

While she'd been falling in love with Zamir she'd been happy, ecstatic.

Because you lived in a fool's paradise.

But now she realised the truth, she couldn't see a way to make this work. She couldn't unsee the truth or pretend everything would be okay. Zamir had shown her how much her self-doubts had held her back. He'd made her appreciate her strengths and in the process made her believe she had a right to happiness. Just as her father had always said.

Her mouth crimped at the corners as the tears she refused to shed burned her eyes and clogged her throat.

Better to know now.

Imagine if you'd had a child together.

The thought paralysed her.

She could imagine it so easily. Longing filled her, so sudden and strong she had to lean into Chico, breathing deep against the aching pleasure-pain of it.

Zamir would love their child as she would. But how would she feel watching the love between father and child grow, knowing Zamir would never love her? That she'd always be a necessary encumbrance. Not wanted for herself. What would she become then? Bitter? Needy? Desperate?

Miranda straightened, stroking Chico's cheek, his ear flicking as she spoke. 'There's only one solution. I have to leave.'

CHAPTER FIFTEEN

'I'M TIRED, ZAMIR. I'll have a bath then go straight to sleep.'

Miranda was already walking towards the bathroom, a vision in deep green silk. But there was an underlying brittleness about her tonight that worried him. Her smile didn't meet her eyes and her shoulders were too high.

No one else had noticed. Their guests at the formal dinner had been delighted and complimentary. Which confirmed how unfounded Miranda's fears had been about not measuring up to royal standards. She was a natural, warm and engaging, interested in everyone. Even if tonight Zamir sensed her mind was elsewhere.

There was something wrong. Something she wasn't sharing.

His nape prickled in alarm. 'What's wrong, Miranda? Has someone said something? Done something?'

There'd been a few grumbles after her first public appearances. A couple of busybodies drawing attention to her less formal manners and foreignness. But most, himself included, found her refreshing. If anything, Zamir was learning from Miranda how to connect more personally with his people. It was time to pull down some of the barriers surrounding the royal family.

'What could be wrong?'

Zamir's heart sank as he watched her gaze dance away from his.

Had she lost weight? Her cheekbones seemed more pronounced and the tight angle of her jaw. But they spent each night naked together. He'd have noticed any weight loss. Which meant it was tension making her look fragile.

He crossed towards her, worried yet sweeping her with an admiring glance. The diamond and emerald necklace he'd given her tonight befitted a queen. But it wasn't the trappings of majesty he responded to. He surveyed her sweet body in the silver-trimmed formal gown of deep emerald-green and need racked him.

'Miranda, I...'

His words dried as she backed a step away from him.

It felt like a stab to the belly. When had his wife ever retreated from him? He slammed to a stop before her.

'Can't it wait? I told you, I'm tired.'

It wasn't the snap of her tone that made him frown. It was the sinking feeling inside. He knew her too well now to be taken in. 'You're not tired. You're trying to avoid talking.'

If anything she looked wired, hyper-alert.

'Talk to me, Miranda. Tell me what's going on.' When she remained silent he dropped his voice to something like a plea. 'We've always been honest with each other.'

Her eyes locked on his and he felt the shock of impact right to the soles of his feet. The familiar sizzle of connection, of sexual awareness and anticipation, and something besides that gathered fear in the pit of his belly and drying throat.

Defeat. Despair. Fear.

Zamir realised that even in those desperate first hours when Miranda had learned the full cost of her decision to kidnap him, she'd never looked like this. Always there'd been a glimmer of fighting spirit in her. Now he looked beyond her show of insouciance into an endless, aching void.

He acted instinctively, covering the space between them and taking her wrists gently, his thumbs stroking her cool skin. She shivered but he couldn't tell whether it was a sensual response to his touch or something else.

'Whatever the problem, we'll fix it.' He bent his head, ensuring she read his determination. 'Between us we'll find a solution.' He curled his mouth in a smile that belied his rising worry. 'Fortunately I've got the resources to help with most things, and after next week's coronation—'

'Don't! Please.' Miranda tugged her hands free and whipped them behind her back.

Zamir frowned. 'Is it the coronation you're worried about? The ceremony is straightforward and, while there'll be a big audience, I know you'll cope. I'm proud of you, Miranda. You've done so well at all your public appearances.'

She shook her head so vehemently, her diamond and emerald earrings swung wide. Below the glittering necklace her breasts rose sharply as if she had trouble catching her breath. He knew the feeling. His lungs felt compressed.

'It's not that. Or only partly that.' She bit her lip and he wanted, so badly, to touch her there and ease the hurt. But—and it killed him to admit to it—twice now she'd withdrawn from him. Once she'd stepped back and later she'd pulled her hands from his as if his touch scalded.

Horror wound through his intestines like a ribbon of ice.

Mirroring her stance, he locked his hands behind his back, signalling that he'd give her the space she wanted.

She looked down then up again, eyes glistening bright, and he realised that for the first time Miranda was on the verge of tears. This was the woman who'd single-handedly kidnapped him. Stood proud and defiant when forced into marriage. Dared to negotiate her own terms for living here. A woman he'd believed utterly fearless.

'Are you sick?' Had she received some terrible diagnosis? 'Or is it someone at home—?'

'It's nothing like that. I'm fine.' She laughed then, a tiny sound that should have reassured yet instead sounded broken, making the fear in him notch higher.

'I didn't want to talk about this tonight when we're both tired. But...' her eyes searched his '...I've realised I can't do this. I really can't. I've tried but it's just not possible long term.'

His voice emerged rough. 'Can't do what precisely?'

Miranda lifted her chin. She owed it to herself to make a stand but when she looked into his stunned eyes she fought the urge to reassure him and promise to try harder.

Didn't that characterise all that was wrong with this marriage? Even knowing this situation would eventually erode her soul, Miranda couldn't help wanting to do what Zamir wanted, try to be the woman he needed.

Because she cared. Too much.

'I can't be your queen. I can't be your wife. I need to get away from all this.'

She snatched a desperate breath ready to forestall his arguments but none came. Zamir stood as if turned to stone. For long seconds he didn't even seem to breathe. Then she saw his chest lift on a shuddering breath.

'It just won't work,' she hurried on. 'It's not working now and it will only get worse.'

Still he said nothing and the sight of him staring down at her, not even angry but lost for words, made her shift her weight from one foot to another.

She shouldn't feel guilty. She hadn't chosen this life. He'd forced her into it.

Yet that argument didn't work against her deep-seated guilt and concern. She had to do this for her survival but she knew her action would cost Zamir enormously. Not just in pride but perhaps in power. That haunted her, making her decision even harder.

She didn't want to hurt him, just save herself.

'I know it will take a long time to unravel this marriage. You said divorce between royals isn't possible but I know if anyone can push change through it's you. I'm willing to wait a few years while you change the law. We don't have to announce our divorce immediately. I can play my part for a while.'

Her throat closed as she imagined pretending in public to be Zamir's partner, while in private they lived separate lives. Even standing close to him now tested her to the limit. It would be easy to give in to Zamir's needs and the craving of her own body, her heart, and stay with him, *be* with him. But that would be self-destructive.

'We can negotiate some arrangement. I could live in

the palace several months a year and attend functions with you.' She waved one hand vaguely. 'And the rest of the time I'll live elsewhere. You won't have to worry about me making headlines with public appearances or scandals. I can live quietly. Maybe at the old house across the border that I inherited.'

She could set up stables there. Even offer riding therapy or do freelance work with other people's horses. Her plans hadn't got that far. Whenever she imagined life after Zamir her mind went blank.

'Why?' he said finally, his voice so strained it was almost unrecognisable. 'Are you really so daunted by the public appearances? If so I could—'

'It's not that.' She didn't find them easy as Zamir did, but she was growing more confident.

'Then what? Do you miss your family? Your home in Argentina? After the coronation we could travel and in the meantime your cousin could visit here.'

Miranda goggled up at him, distracted for a moment from her misery. 'You'd have Sadia here?' The woman who'd plotted kidnap rather than marry him?

'I'll do whatever it takes to make you happy here, Miranda. To make you feel comfortable.'

Behind her back her hands twisted together. His earnest words reinforced what Sadia had said. That Zamir wanted her happy so she could play the part of his bride.

The sad thing was she'd be immeasurably happy without all the trappings of royalty, if only Zamir loved her.

She shook her head. 'Don't, Zamir. There's nothing you can say that will make things right. You're a good man. You mean well and I…like you. But being here, pretending to be happy… I just can't do it for the rest of my life.'

Miranda looked into his solemn features, the twitch of a frown between his eyebrows, the confusion in his eyes, and felt obliged to explain.

'I don't expect you to understand. You were raised to expect an arranged marriage. But I want, *need* something more.'

She smoothed damp palms down her long skirt. 'Most of my life I felt second best. The first five years of my life were gloriously happy. But after my father died I never measured up to expectations. I bounced from one place to another, one set of customs and expectations and another. I tried to be what my mother wanted but I disappointed her. I gave up trying to please my uncle years ago. In Argentina I had a career I loved. But I was still an outsider.'

She shook her head. 'Maybe I always will be. But I've learnt, and you helped me realise this, that I want and deserve respect and love. Because of who I am as a person. Not because of other people's expectations or needs.'

Miranda clasped her hands in an unconsciously pleading gesture. 'If I stay here I'll always be the wife you had to have. The stand-in bride. Not the one you chose. I'll never be *loved*.'

She ground to a halt as the words spilled out.

Then, on a surge of recklessness, she added, 'You might be able to live without love, Zamir, but I'm not made that way. When you were kind to me and caring it meant so much. It made me realise I crave genuine emotion in a relationship. It made me realise how needy I'd become and how much I'd put up with over the years. I can't be that woman any longer and I'm sorry, so sorry. I'll do whatever it takes to put an end to this farce of a marriage but I need my freedom.'

Because staying with the man she loved in this unequal relationship would turn her into a shadow of herself.

'Please, let's talk later. I need time alone.'

Miranda's eyes went to the exit to her old suite, but Zamir was between her and it. Instead she spun on her foot and hurried into the bathroom.

CHAPTER SIXTEEN

ZAMIR STARED AT the closed door, reeling.

She believed what they shared was a farce?

Pain speared him, from his chest down to feet that refused to move.

He'd tried so hard, given so much. How could she dismiss the amazing things they'd shared?

Did they really mean nothing to her?

He would have sworn on his soul that she'd also experienced those times of pure communion that transcended the reality of two separate beings. Those moments when it felt they were one, not just physically but mentally and emotionally.

Zamir had never known such a bond or such peace.

It made him realise there was far more to life than duty, despite the dictates of his uncle and his own habit of tunnel-visioned focus.

He cared about Miranda, worked hard to help her adjust, even opening up about his family life and past with her. He'd never done that before. He'd believed, despite the short time they'd been together, that they'd built an unparalleled level of trust and affection.

Now she wanted her freedom?

Anger stirred. She'd taken everything he offered and dismissed it out of hand.

Didn't she understand the freedom he gave her, the freedom she could take for herself as his queen?

But that wasn't good enough, apparently.

He wasn't good enough.

She wanted love on top of everything else. The full romantic dream.

What did she expect? Vows on bended knee? She already has his respect and affection.

But Zamir knew nothing about romantic love. It had never figured in his family as far as he could tell. It was something that happened to other people, as distant from his world as the moon.

Zamir's clenched jaw grew slack. His mind raced. His vision narrowed to the intricate inlay work on the door before him, but he didn't register it.

A great weight crushed his chest and his lungs fought to drag in enough air.

Still he stood, rooted to the spot, blood pounding, thoughts whirling, hands clenched into fists.

Miranda wanted the impossible.

The man who'd been brought up to be responsible and dutiful, bound by the dictates of the public good over personal preference, was stunned.

Yet another part of him applauded her for standing up for what she believed she needed. His heart had cracked as she'd admitted to feeling second best. To feeling she didn't belong.

Did she fear she was unworthy of the love she craved?

What would it be like to admit what it was *he* wanted from life? To build a future tailored to make that possible?

Zamir had some idea. He'd encouraged his siblings to pursue their dreams. He'd understood that neither of them wanted the burden he carried, of statesmanship and constant expectation. He revelled in their successes.

Yet he couldn't revel in Miranda's determination to plot her own course and seek her own joys.

Because you want her to find joy with you.

You want her too much to let her go.

Because even after this short time together you can't imagine going back to a life without her.

When the door opened, the room was lit by a single lamp. Miranda paused on the threshold, gripping the neckline of her robe close, cautiously surveying the room. Her face was scrubbed bare of make-up, she wore no adornment but her golden wedding band, and she'd never looked more lovely.

Was it his sharply indrawn breath that caught her attention, or did she sense him in the shadows?

One step into the room she paused, head turning unerringly to where he sat on the window seat.

'Zamir?'

'Who else did you expect?'

It hit him that, if Miranda got her way and they lived separate lives, one day some other man would share the intimacy of midnight conversations. And more, much more. His pain grew excruciating.

He rose. 'We need to speak.'

'It's very late. Let's talk tomorrow.'

Zamir rolled his shoulders, trying to unknot the tension there. 'No. This is too important. You had your say. Now it's my turn.'

For the longest time she hesitated, then with a tiny

nod she crossed the room, her expression guarded. 'I'm sorry, Zamir. Truly sorry.'

Sorry! A tide of fury and fear rose at her decision to desert him. But he pushed it down. He couldn't let emotions control him now. He needed to get this right.

He gestured for her to take one end of the long, cushioned window seat. When she did, he sat at the other end, turning to face her.

The lamplight left this part of the room in shadows but the moon was out and he could see her features. They were so familiar he could almost read them in the dark anyway. One good look told him she suffered too. Regret as well as anxiety were in the way she folded and refolded the silk of her robe. And there was pain around her mouth and eyes.

His anger crumbled. Pride had no place here. He wanted to reach out to her but instinct told him she needed far more than physical reassurance.

Besides, this wasn't just about Miranda. It was about *them*. No wonder he was on edge. He had no margin for error.

'I've been thinking.' He shook his head as his carefully planned words fled, replaced by such banality.

Zamir swallowed, fighting to conquer his own apprehension. He wasn't a man given to anxiety. He was used to decision-making and high-stakes negotiation but nothing in his experience had prepared him for this.

'What you said tonight has made me reassess.'

'You're rethinking our marriage? You'll organise a divorce?' Strangely, Miranda didn't sound thrilled.

Was he grasping at straws?

'Not rethinking our marriage. Reassessing my priorities.' He paused, struggling with words to explain. Discussing emotions was new to him. 'You explained what you wanted from life, what was important. I respect you for being honest.' Even if it came as a crushing blow. 'It made me think about *my* feelings and needs.'

Silence stretched between them. Had he thought she'd help him out?

She doesn't know what you feel. How could she when you didn't even know yourself?

Zamir looked at his hands, bunched fists on his thighs. 'That's a luxury I never indulged in before.' He looked up to see her lean closer. 'All my life my role was mapped out for me. What's expected of me. The need to be strong, decisive, proud but not selfish. The need to put my nation first. But tonight I feel selfish. I want to be able to claim what *I* want. As if I were an ordinary citizen.'

'What do you want, Zamir?'

It was a whisper, so soft he couldn't read Miranda's tone. It gave no clue to her thoughts, which meant the admission he was about to make would take him into uncharted territory, putting his real self on the line, probably to be rejected.

No wonder he was petrified. These new feelings had the power to destroy.

He grimaced. 'Nothing outlandish. Probably what everyone else wants, including you. I want to be happy. But happiness doesn't come from my title or position.' Though he enjoyed helping people and was proud of his ability to do so. 'I want someone to share my life with. Not because it's decreed or because it brings political advantage. But because that person cares for me. I want love too.'

The words sounded foreign on his tongue yet they felt right.

His heart pounded like a jackhammer, making it impossible to hear anything Miranda said. But Zamir was watching her and she said nothing, though her mouth sagged in astonishment.

A good sign? Or an indication she thought it impossible anyone could love him?

'You made me think about what it is to be loved. It's not something I'd considered before, because I never saw the need. But things have changed. *I've* changed.' It astonished him how much.

'To me love covers respect, admiration, trust, and attraction…deep, deep attraction.' Despite his tension he smiled. 'It's about being there for the other person no matter what. It's about mutual support and affection. Wanting your partner to be the best version of themselves they can be, not managing them so they're forced into a mould they don't fit. It's about sharing joys and pain, whatever life brings.'

Still Miranda said nothing, but as he peered at her in the gloom he saw something silvery on her cheek.

'Miranda?' He leaned forward, brushing away the only tear he'd ever seen her shed. His chest squeezed so hard it was a wonder he breathed. 'I didn't mean to upset you.'

He had no idea what to do. He'd thought she wanted honesty, full emotional honesty. Instead he'd hurt her.

She shook her head, drawing his hand from her cheek. 'You didn't. You just described it so perfectly it made me feel…'

Zamir heard her words through a blare of triumph because she still held his hand. Surely that was a good sign.

'There's a reason I can describe it so well,' he murmured, sliding closer. 'I'm in love with you.'

He waited for the sky to fall in or for her to laugh disbelievingly. Instead her fingers clutched his and her bright eyes held his. Hope trickled through him.

'Tell me.'

It was too soft to be a command, yet he heard his own urgency in Miranda's words.

'I didn't realise it until you said your piece then flounced into the bathroom.'

'I've never flounced.'

Her indignation settled some of his nerves, even though everything still hung in the balance. 'Flounced,' he repeated. 'Just like you sashay into a room when you're wearing something particularly sexy and you know I'm alone. Don't try to deny it. I enjoy it.' The rough, gravel note of his voice gave him away. He tried to lighten the atmosphere because his feelings were so big they threatened to overwhelm him.

What had happened to the man who kept personal emotions locked away?

'You made me wonder exactly what you meant by wanting love. I tried to define it for myself, break it down into components so I could understand.'

Zamir drew a slow breath, mustering his courage. He clasped her hand in both his.

'That's when I realised I was in love with you. I'd never thought about love and romance before, I was too busy worrying about responsibilities and expectations. But as soon as I stopped to consider I realised that you're the only woman I want in my life. It's not about being a suitable queen, though you're that and more. You have your own style and you're superb. But I'd feel the same if I weren't Sheikh. I crave you and suspect I always will, but it's more than that. I admire you. I enjoy debating with you, even arguing. I care about you.' He leaned closer, willing her to understand. 'I want to share your life and have you beside me through mine. I want…*us*.'

'Oh, Zamir!' She shook her head. 'I want to believe you. I know you'd never deliberately lie. But this revelation is very convenient. Maybe you're imagining feelings because you know I want to leave.'

His heart bottomed out. Everything went into free fall.

She wanted love, but not *his* love.

The pain was inconceivably sharp. A honed, heated blade scoring his skin before plunging deeper.

His royal education had taught him many things but rejection wasn't one of them. He couldn't even seem to let go of her hand, still clasping it in his.

With an effort, Zamir pushed back his shoulders and sat straighter. He hadn't finished. He'd come this far, he owed it to himself to continue.

'Convenient isn't the word I'd use.' Another breath, another stabbing pain. 'Contrary to what you think, I *do* mean it. So much that if there's a chance you feel the same about me, I'm willing to walk away from the coronation.'

He heard her hiss of shock but kept going. 'I don't need to be Sheikh to be happy. I can still work for my country, still contribute in other ways if it means you'll feel free to love me back.'

The world seemed to freeze with his words. Everything stilled except the quick thud-thud of his pulse and the fine tremor in Miranda's hand.

'You'd abdicate?' Her voice wobbled on the word.

'Technically it's not abdication if I haven't been formally crowned.'

Miranda clung to his hands, leaning so close he caught a drift of her sweet jasmine scent with its underlying note of warm, womanly flesh. His nostrils flared greedily.

'I don't care what it's called! You're saying you'd leave all this behind if I wanted it?'

'If you wanted me. If you loved me.'

The tremor in her hands became a shudder.

He shouldn't but he couldn't help hoping that was a positive. At least she wasn't indifferent.

'You can't do that.' She sounded angry. 'It's who you are, what you've trained for all your life. You're good at it and you enjoy it.'

Zamir shrugged. 'I told you once before that I didn't want the crown for personal reasons. It's a vocation that was thrust on me. I could be as happy working for my country in another way, if I had you.'

He'd just laid his heart, his happiness and his future bare. He'd deliberately made himself vulnerable. It terrified him yet at the same time felt incredibly liberating. Because now he and Miranda were just a man and woman, equals. That was what he craved.

'But you said your brother didn't want to be Sheikh. If you left he'd be forced to take the role.'

She was more worried about Umar than him? His tentative pleasure dimmed. 'My brother is a grown man. It would be his choice. And if he chose not then someone else would be found.'

'But they wouldn't find anyone as good as you. They need you.'

Zamir withdrew his hands and shot to his feet. If all Miranda could worry about was who led his country, it was clear she didn't return his feelings.

'They'd make do.' He paused, knowing he had to say it, yet rejecting the idea with every atom in his body. 'I told you how I feel about you, Miranda. The fact you haven't returned the favour tells me all I need to know. I wish you goodnight.'

He was halfway across the room when she rushed across to stand before him, hectic colour in her cheeks.

'You really mean it!'

Zamir scowled. 'You think I'd joke about something like this?'

'No, I don't think you would.' She planted her hands on his chest, fingers splayed, leaning so close he automatically wrapped his arms around her. Almost automatically, for he was desperate for one last hug, if that was what this was. 'I just never thought... You don't do anything by halves, do you? I like your decisiveness, but this…!'

'Oh, so there's something about me you like?'

'Love. Things I *love* about you. Why do you think I was so desperate to leave? I fell in love with you and couldn't bear to be just your necessary wife. Not when you mean everything to me.'

A great sunburst of joy exploded inside Zamir. His arms tightened around her, pulling her hard against him. As ever, they felt perfect together.

For a long time he said nothing, his throat too tight to speak, his heart overflowing.

'You *are* my necessary wife,' he managed finally. 'I couldn't go on without you, Miranda. You believe me, don't you?'

Her head tilted and her hands slid up to cup his face as if learning its contours anew. 'I really do. It's amazing, incredible, but I do.'

'*You're* amazing and incredible.'

Her laughter was throaty, spiralling through his vital organs and easing the unbearable strain in his muscles.

'So what's it to be, my love?' Had any two words ever sounded as good as those? 'Marriage to a Sheikh or an ordinary citizen?'

Her expression was warm and for the first time Zamir saw love, complete and unfettered, reflected back at him. It was a wondrous moment he'd remember for the rest of his days.

'To a Sheikh, of course. You'll be the best leader this country has ever had.'

'Even if it means we have to live in the palace and follow protocol at least some of the time?'

Her smile was mischievous. 'I can put up with that if it means being with you. Besides, think of the perks. Sheikhs have the biggest, most comfortable beds and plenty of money to invest in the best stables.'

Gravely he nodded, fighting a grin. 'I'm glad you finally saw sense.' Then in a single, satisfying move, he lifted her into his arms.

'Not sense.' Her words feathered his chin. 'Love. True love.'

Zamir paused on the way to that big, royal bed. He looked into her lustrous eyes, his heart expanding with pure joy. 'True love.' It was a vow. 'Now and for ever.'

EPILOGUE

'YOU REALLY KNOW how to throw a party, Miranda. This is much better than any palace reception I remember.'

'Really?'

She turned from her sister-in-law beside her on the secluded balcony, to survey the crowd below them in the huge courtyard. She'd thought the space with its wide, paved areas, fragrant shrubs and decorative water features perfect for an evening reception. But it had never been used for a public event before.

After two years with Zamir, Miranda was much more comfortable suggesting changes to palace arrangements, but it was good to have her ideas endorsed so wholeheartedly.

'Absolutely. The grand reception halls are fine for state occasions but this is much more relaxed and welcoming. And I approve the more varied guest list. Not just the privileged and the powerful. In fact I had a fascinating conversation earlier with someone about irrigation improvements.' Afifa craned her neck. 'There he is. I'm just going to catch him again. There's something I want to check.'

She threaded her way past a knot of diplomats and a European prince who was in deep conversation with

Miranda's stepfather, and one of the young men who had participated in that first diversionary programme in the royal stables. Far from following a career in crime, he was working with horses full-time and planning to train as a vet.

'They're probably discussing polo,' murmured a deep voice near her shoulder as a hand slid around hers.

Miranda smiled and leaned against her husband as their fingers threaded together. Her heart lifted as it always did near him. 'Of course they are. Meanwhile Afifa has met another agronomist and they're talking shop.'

'And did you notice Umar and Sadia?'

Miranda nodded, locating them, heads together, on the edge of the crowd. 'Since he decided to do a documentary on early childhood development they spend a lot of time together. Do you mind?'

She turned, looking up into the honed, proud features of the man she loved. His ebony stare caressed like velvet and promised private delight when the reception ended. A shiver of anticipation unfurled lazily inside.

Zamir shook his head, eyes not leaving hers. 'They seem well matched. Sadia's blossomed into an interesting woman these last couple of years.'

Miranda nodded but her attention wasn't on her cousin. A finger stroked the centre of her palm, making her nipples bead against her scarlet dress.

'Did I tell you how beautiful you look tonight?' Zamir's voice dropped to that intimate note that made her blood pump faster and her skin tighten.

'Only once or twice.'

He bent close, his words caressing her cheek. 'How remiss. You're utterly gorgeous. And...' His mouth curved into a sensual smile that undid something inside her. 'You're all mine.'

'And you're mine.'

'As if I'd ever forget.' His voice dropped even lower. 'I have plans for you once this reception is over...*wife*.'

A thrill passed through her. Miranda loved the way he called her that. With delicious intent and deep, abiding love.

'Excellent. I have plans for you too...*husband*. I want to renegotiate our agreement.'

Zamir lifted one eyebrow, that carnal smile still curling the corners of his mouth. 'Do you, indeed? Which part of our agreement?'

'The bit about not having children yet.'

Miranda would never forget watching his expression change from amusement to astonishment, elation and, as ever, love.

'Don't get too excited. We may not even be able to—'

'I know. Time will tell, but the fact that you want to try...' His smile was crooked and his voice gravelly. 'You really *do* trust me.'

His cheeks were warm beneath her palms as she leaned close. 'Of course I do.' How could he think anything else?

Zamir gathered her to him, his embrace gentle. 'Miranda, you're my love, the other half of my heart.'

Then, ignoring protocol and the possibility that someone might look up to the shadowy balcony, he kissed her with all the ardent tenderness she could wish for.

When finally they pulled apart, she whispered, 'You know, the best decision I ever made was to kidnap you.'

Zamir's laugh made heads turn as they walked hand in hand to join their guests.

* * * * *

Did you get caught up in the drama of
His Last-Minute Desert Queen?
*Then you're bound to fall in love
with these other stories
by Annie West!*

The Desert King Meets His Match
Reclaiming His Runaway Cinderella
Reunited by the Greek's Baby
The Housekeeper and the Brooding Billionaire
Nine Months to Save Their Marriage

Available now!

#4177 CINDERELLA'S ONE-NIGHT BABY
by Michelle Smart

A glamorous evening at the palace with Spanish tycoon Andrés? Irresistible! Even if Gabrielle knows this one encounter is all the guarded Spaniard will allow himself. Yet, when the chemistry simmering between them erupts into mind-blowing passion, the nine-month consequence will tie her and Andrés together forever...

#4178 HIDDEN HEIR WITH HIS HOUSEKEEPER
A Diamond in the Rough
by Heidi Rice

Self-made billionaire Mason Foxx would never forget the sizzling encounter he had with society princess Bea Medford. But his empire comes first, always. Until months later, he gets the ultimate shock: Bea isn't just the housekeeper at the hotel he's staying at—she's also carrying his child!

#4179 THE SICILIAN'S DEAL FOR "I DO"
Brooding Billionaire Brothers
by Clare Connelly

Marriage offered Mia Marini distance from her oppressive family, so Luca Cavallaro's desertion of their convenient wedding devastated her, especially after their mind-blowing kiss! Then Luca returns with a scandalous proposition: risk it all for a no-strings week together...and claim the wedding night they never had!

#4180 PREGNANCY CLAUSE IN THEIR PAPER MARRIAGE
by Kate Hewitt

Honoring the strict rules of his on-paper marriage, Christos Diakis has fought hard to ignore the electricity simmering between him and his wife, Lana. Her request that they have a baby rocks the very foundations of their union. And Christos has neither the power—nor wish—to decline...

#4181 THE FORBIDDEN BRIDE HE STOLE
by Millie Adams

Hannah will do *anything* to avoid the magnetic pull of her guardian, Apollo, including marry another. Then Apollo shockingly steals her from the altar, and a dangerous flame is ignited. Hannah must decide—is their passion a firestorm she can survive unscathed, or will it burn everything down?

#4182 AWAKENED IN HER ENEMY'S PALAZZO
by Kim Lawrence

Grace Stewart never expected to inherit a palazzo from her beloved late employer. Or that his ruthless tech mogul son, Theo Ranieri, would move in until she agrees to sell! Sleeping under the same roof fuels their agonizing attraction. There's just one place their standoff can end—in Theo's bed!

#4183 THE KING SHE SHOULDN'T CRAVE
by Lela May Wight

Promoted from spare to heir after tragedy struck, Angelo can't be distracted from his duty. Being married to the woman he has always craved—his brother's intended queen—has him on the precipice of self-destruction. The last thing he needs is for Natalia to recognize their dangerous attraction. If she does, there's nothing to stop it from becoming all-consuming...

#4184 UNTOUCHED UNTIL THE GREEK'S RETURN
by Susan Stephens

Innocent Rosy Bloom came to Greece looking for peace. But there's nothing peaceful about the storm of desire tycoon Xander Tsakis unleashes in her upon his return to his island home! Anything they share would be temporary, but Xander's dangerously thrilling proximity has cautious Rosy abandoning all reason!

YOU CAN FIND MORE INFORMATION ON UPCOMING HARLEQUIN TITLES, FREE EXCERPTS AND MORE AT HARLEQUIN.COM.

HPCNMRB0124

Get 3 FREE REWARDS!

We'll send you 2 FREE Books <u>plus</u> a FREE Mystery Gift.

FREE Value Over **$20**

Both the **Harlequin® Desire** and **Harlequin Presents®** series feature compelling
novels filled with passion, sensuality and intriguing scandals.

YES! Please send me 2 FREE novels from the Harlequin Desire or Harlequin Presents
series and my FREE gift (gift is worth about $10 retail). After receiving them, if I don't
wish to receive any more books, I can return the shipping statement marked "cancel."
If I don't cancel, I will receive 6 brand-new Harlequin Presents Larger-Print books
every month and be billed just $6.30 each in the U.S. or $6.49 each in Canada, a
savings of at least 10% off the cover price, or 3 Harlequin Desire books (2-in-1 story
editions) every month and be billed just $7.83 each in the U.S. or $8.43 each in
Canada, a savings of at least 12% off the cover price. It's quite a bargain! Shipping
and handling is just 50¢ per book in the U.S. and $1.25 per book in Canada.* I
understand that accepting the 2 free books and gift places me under no obligation
to buy anything. I can always return a shipment and cancel at any time by calling
the number below. The free books and gift are mine to keep no matter what I decide.

Choose one: ☐ **Harlequin Desire**
(225/326 BPA GRNA)

☐ **Harlequin
Presents
Larger-Print**
(176/376 BPA GRNA)

☐ **Or Try Both!**
(225/326 & 176/376
BPA GRQP)

Name (please print)

Address   Apt. #

City   State/Province   Zip/Postal Code

Email: Please check this box ☐ if you would like to receive newsletters and promotional emails from Harlequin Enterprises ULC and
its affiliates. You can unsubscribe anytime.

Mail to the **Harlequin Reader Service:**
IN U.S.A.: P.O. Box 1341, Buffalo, NY 14240-8531
IN CANADA: P.O. Box 603, Fort Erie, Ontario L2A 5X3

Want to try 2 free books from another series? Call 1-800-873-8635 or visit www.ReaderService.com.

*Terms and prices subject to change without notice. Prices do not include sales taxes, which will be charged (if applicable) based
on your state or country of residence. Canadian residents will be charged applicable taxes. Offer not valid in Quebec. This offer is
limited to one order per household. Books received may not be as shown. Not valid for current subscribers to the Harlequin Presents
or Harlequin Desire series. All orders subject to approval. Credit or debit balances in a customer's account(s) may be offset by any
other outstanding balance owed by or to the customer. Please allow 4 to 6 weeks for delivery. Offer available while quantities last.

Your Privacy—Your information is being collected by Harlequin Enterprises ULC, operating as Harlequin Reader Service. For a
complete summary of the information we collect, how we use this information and to whom it is disclosed, please visit our privacy notice
located at corporate.harlequin.com/privacy-notice. From time to time we may also exchange your personal information with reputable
third parties. If you wish to opt out of this sharing of your personal information, please visit readerservice.com/consumerchoice or
call 1-800-873-8635. **Notice to California Residents**—Under California law, you have specific rights to control and access your data.
For more information on these rights and how to exercise them, visit corporate.harlequin.com/california-privacy.

HDHP23